MW01168465

Otherworldly: Volume 1
A Genre Fiction Anthology
Nerd Street

Lucy's Lantern Literature with Nerd Street

Contents

BEN WOLF

Award–Winning Multi–Genre Author

Author Ben Wolf

BEN WOLF is an award-winning author of fantasy, sci-fi, horror, and children's books. When not writing, he plays video games and chokes his friends in Brazilian jiu jitsu. You can follow him on Facebook in the Ben Wolfpack or check out his author website, **www.benwolf.com**. Aeron and Wafer's story continues in Blood Mercenaries Origins, Book Zero of Ben Wolf's acclaimed Blood Mercenaries sword & sorcery series. Get it now—FOR FREE—at: **www.subscribepage.com/fantasy-readers**

Chapter One

Leatherwing – A Blood Mercenaries Short Story

By: Ben Wolf

Aeron Ironglade lay on the battlefield, pinned under his own horse.

Around him, fellow Govalian soldiers clashed against an army of rebels. Shouts and clangs resonated across the field, and black smoke billowed from scattered patches of burning grain.

High above, dozens of winged silhouettes streaked across the sky—the Govalian Wyvern Knight Corps, dropping from the ether to rain havoc upon their enemies. But they were too far away to help Aeron.

Two javelins had turned Aeron's horse into a thousand-pound pincushion, and now his own spear lay just beyond his grasp. His left leg ached, unquestionably anchored beneath his horse. At least it wasn't broken—or at least, it didn't *feel* broken.

If Aeron couldn't get free, one of the rebels would eventually find him and finish him off. Then he'd never see Mum and Kallie again.

Aeron struggled and pushed and squirmed, but he couldn't get his leg free.

If it would budge just a little bit, I might be able to—

Footsteps thudded behind him, accompanied by the singing of steel.

A fellow Govalian soldier, clad in the infantry's traditional forest-green armor, battled an rebel who wore mishmash of leather and iron.

They fought twenty feet from Aeron's position, with the Govalian's soldier's back to Aeron, as if defending him. Whether or not it was intentional, Aeron cast silent prayers for the soldier.

Apparently, the gods weren't listening. The rebel's dark blade, tainted orange with rust and streaked with dirt and blood, cut down the Govalian soldier in three decisive hacks. Blood from the final blow spattered on the rebel's bearded face, sharpening the savagery in his dark eyes.

Then those bloodthirsty eyes found Aeron's.

So much for the gods' favor. Aeron shoved against the dead husk of horse again, but he still couldn't move it.

The rebel stalked closer. A twisted smile parted his bloodstained lips.

Aeron both cursed and begged the gods' favor again. He couldn't die now, in his first real battle, because of bad luck and a dead horse weighing him down.

More importantly, he couldn't let Pa be right about him. He had to prove he wasn't destined to be a failure forever.

Panic raked Aeron's nerves, and he pushed for his very life, desperate to get free.

The horse wouldn't budge.

As the rebel drew nearer, wing beats thundered overhead. Aeron's heart leaped with hope, but only briefly.

Unhindered by the sounds and the shadow now looming over them, the battle-crazed rebel hefted his chipped sword high.

Aeron raised his arms to shield himself.

Then a massive black form slammed into the rebel from above and smashed him into the earth. The rebel wailed as its scaly black reptilian tale lashed back and forth.

The wyvern had pinned the rebel to the ground, and its taloned toes dug into the flesh of the man's thigh. The wyvern's vicious teeth tore into the rebel's chest as he screamed and flailed, his menacing sword now worthless.

The knight atop the winged beast wore dark-gray armor and a matching helmet. He held a spear in one hand and gripped one of the wyvern's golden horn-like bones ridging its back with his other. A small golden insignia—a wyvern wing—was stamped onto the left shoulder of his armor.

The wyvern itself was equally impressive—and huge. Striking golden stripes traced down the beast's sides from its head down to the tip of its tail, which boasted a spike of golden bone like those along its back.

For a moment, Aeron wondered if the emperor himself had come to his aid. As the wyvern continued to thrash and shred the rebel's body with its jaws and rear talons, the knight atop the wyvern looked down at Aeron.

It was the first time Aeron had been so close to a wyvern knight. He realized he knew the man seated atop the wyvern, if only by reputation. He'd just been saved by one of the greatest knights the Govalian Empire had ever known—General Cadimus himself.

Aeron would've marveled at him even if he hadn't been the general, but the realization awakened something inside Aeron—something unique and pro-found. Something new.

A purpose.

The wyvern stopped ravaging the rebel's body—he was beyond dead at this point—and turned back toward Aeron. General Cadimus and the yellow-eyed wyvern stared down at Aeron. Blood dripped from the beast's teeth and snout, and then its head lashed down at him.

Aeron flinched, but no pain came. When he dared to look up again, he saw the wyvern's jaws latched onto the neck of the dead horse and began to effortlessly pull it up. The redistribution of the horse's weight pinched Aeron's leg briefly, but soon he was free.

He scrambled to his feet, snatched up his spear, and turned back to thank General Cadimus for his aid, but they'd already taken to the air in a whirlwind of wing beats, leaving Aeron behind.

As he watched the wyvern fly away, that sense of purpose resurged in Aeron's chest.

I'm gonna be a wyvern knight, too. Aeron granted himself a grin, even amid the carnage of the battlefield around him. *That'll be me someday. I swear it will be.*

Another rebel lumbered toward Aeron from several yards away, wielding a weatherworn woodcutter's axe.

Aeron raised his spear. *But first I have to survive this battle.*

He rushed forward and met the rebel in the fray.

Three Years Later

"In closing, I hereby commission the 271st Featherwing Class to serve your emperor and his army faithfully." General Cadimus's voice boomed across the fortress courtyard.

Aeron Ironglade glanced at the beautiful girl with the slightly pointed ears and short white-blonde hair. She stood four spots to his left and one row ahead of him.

Some sort of elf, maybe?

He'd noticed her before General Cadimus's speech that afternoon, and now that he'd seen her, Aeron had to keep forcing himself to look away.

"You are not merely the next wave of potential knights to join our esteemed Wyvern Knight Corps," General Cadimus continued, "you represent our nation's great hope for a more prosperous and secure future."

General Cadimus surveyed the group of Featherwings with a hawk-eyed stare. Salt-and-pepper hair flowed from his scalp to his shoulders, and a matching beard, long but neatly trimmed, covered the lower half of his face.

But as magnificent as that beard was, and despite General Cadimus's stalwart gaze, Aeron's focus shifted to the blonde girl again.

She wore the same forest-green armor as the rest of the recruits, but rather than a steel-colored horse head stamped into the metal of her right shoulder like the one on Aeron's, a steel bow and arrow marked hers instead.

He'd never heard of an archer making the jump to the Wyvern Knight Corps. Usually, prospects came from the cavalry, like him. Transitioning from riding a horse to riding a wyvern made a lot more sense than shooting a bunch of arrows all day.

Maybe she's a bad archer, Aeron mused. *Maybe they sent her here to get rid of her.*

The girl glanced back at him with striking blue eyes, and Aeron had no problem averting his gaze then—though he might've caught a hint of a smirk on her face before he did. It made him want to grin, but he stifled it in case she was still looking. When he checked again, she wasn't.

General Cadimus continued, "But make no mistake: your training will be rigorous. Every task you face will challenge your skills and expand your understanding of combat atop these majestic creatures..."

A high-pitched whistle sounded from somewhere distant, so shrill that Aeron almost didn't hear it at all. The girl, however, flinched and covered her pointed ears until it subsided.

Definitely some sort of elf. Aeron squinted at her. With those ears and that hair, she had to be. *But why would an elf join the Govalian army?*

A cacophony of furious wing beats truncated Aeron's thoughts. High above, dozens of black forms filled the sunlit sky. The sight stole Aeron's breath, and it took him back to that day on the battlefield three years earlier.

The Wyvern Knight Corps. The elite of the Govalian Army.

If Aeron passed the training and managed to bond with a newly hatched wyvern, he could become one of them. A Leatherwing. A full-fledged wyvern knight.

He'd wanted nothing else since General Cadimus saved him that day on the battlefield. Now, at long last, he'd get his chance to make it a reality.

But as Aeron watched the skies, he realized he'd been wrong. There weren't dozens of them—there were *hundreds*.

He'd assumed that only the wyverns based at the fortress had shown up for the induction ceremony, but given how many now flew overhead, he'd either severely underestimated the size of the wyverns' roost, or other fortresses and outposts had sent their wyvern knights back for the ceremony.

A spectrum of blues, greens, browns, and even reds and oranges colored many of the wyverns' scales. Some had stripes or discolored patches along their flanks. Others actually *were* black or gray, but they seemed rare compared the overwhelming number of wyverns in the blue-to-green range.

As the wyvern knights circled overhead, General Cadimus concluded, "May you fly together toward the adventure that lies beyond the horizon of the Govalian Empire, from the portal to the Aetherworld to the gates of the Underworld and back again, wreathed in the glory you have rightfully earned. Go forth, and make your country proud."

As General Cadimus stepped back, the gold wyvern wing stamped on his left shoulder glinted in the sun, stark against his dark-gray armor. For a few seconds, Aeron wondered if Pa had forged General Cadimus's armor.

Then a massive winged form, black with familiar gold stripes, landed next to General Cadimus with a thud that shook the ground under Aeron's feet.

It was the biggest, most imposing beast in the Wyvern Knight Corps. Aeron didn't know its name, but he'd never forget its distinct coloration and its cunning yellow eyes.

General Cadimus donned his dark-gray helmet, mounted his wyvern, and took to the sky in a flurry of wing beats that showered the Featherwings in the courtyard with dust.

Aeron shielded his eyes, and when the storm ceased, the Featherwings around him began to break their orderly ranks, eager to get in line for the forthcoming induction feast.

He scanned the Featherwings around him for the blonde maybe-elf girl, but she was nowhere to be found.

Aeron couldn't remember how he'd made it to his bunk inside the fortress barracks that night, but he woke up to shouting and a mammoth headache pounding his head.

Definitely overdid it last night.

His first four years of training with the Govalian Army—one year with the infantry and the last three with the cavalry—kicked in, and he dragged himself to his feet and stood at attention.

At first, the noise hit his ears as meaningless blaring, but the more his headache sharpened, the more the words crystallized. The words hammered at him just as relentlessly.

"...your armor on, and rendezvous in the courtyard."

Wasn't I just there? Aeron moaned. It felt like he'd only slept for a couple of hours. He still hadn't dared to open his eyes. Maybe if he didn't, he'd be able to go back to sleep.

"*You*," a voice snapped at Aeron only inches from his face, and his eyes popped open.

"Sir." Aeron's training reignited, and though his vision refused to focus on the face of the black-haired officer that stood before him, his ears worked fine now.

"You're wobbling." The voice had an Urthian accent to it, which Aeron found strange. "Straighten your back. Steady yourself. Have you always been a disgrace?"

Aeron bristled. This guy was being a jerk, so Aeron decided to fire back.

"Only until yesterday, sir. Now I'm the 'nation's great hope for a more prosperous and secure future,'" he parroted the line from General Cadimus's speech.

The commander's stern face did not change. "This is your first day as a Featherwing. Do you intend to fail before your training even begins?"

Aeron's vision sharpened, and he took in the officer's smug face and his long black hair—and the silver wyvern wing stamped on the left shoulder of his dark-gray armor. This guy was a commander, a Silverwing, meaning he reported directly to General Cadimus.

Aeron willed his body to go rigid as an anvil. Maybe he'd better be more careful. "No, sir."

"What's your name, Featherwing?" the commander asked.

"Ironglade, sir," he replied. "Aeron Ironglade."

"Featherwing Ironglade, suit up and report to the courtyard with the rest of the inductees. Anyone not present for roll call in ten minutes will be removed from consideration immediately." Then the commander addressed everyone else in the barracks, "Crystal?"

In unison with the others, Aeron bellowed, "Clear, sir!"

"Then *get moving.*"

As the first rays of sunlight crested the courtyard walls, Aeron and about forty other Featherwings gathered in the courtyard. Now clad in his armor, including his cavalry helmet, Aeron shivered in the early morning spring temperatures.

Aeron's armor weighed plenty, but it did little to keep him warm. If he ever went back home, perhaps he'd talk to Pa about finding a way to make warmer armor.

If he ever went back home. And *if* he ever talked to Pa again.

The commander who'd summoned everyone emerged from within the fortress. Behind him walked two Steelwings—mid-ranking officers in the Wyvern Knight Corps—who led two lines of Featherwing initiates behind them. A few of them wore full armor, but most wore only some of it.

All of them stared down at their feet as they walked into the courtyard and stopped in two separate lines before the majority of the Featherwings.

"My name is Commander Larcas Brove," the commander began. "I oversee the day-to-day operations of the Wyvern Knight Corps here in central Govalia. From now on, I am the sole arbiter of your fates."

Great. Aeron's stomach soured at the thought.

"These sad wretches before you failed to make it to the courtyard on time," Commander Brove continued. "As such, they have forfeited their opportunity to join the Wyvern Knight Corps. They will not receive another."

Aeron scanned their faces, searching for the blonde girl, hoping he wouldn't find her. He didn't see her among the Featherwings being kicked out, so he tried to steal a glance at the ranks around him.

"*Ironglade,*" Commander Brove snapped. "Am I boring you?"

"No, sir." Aeron's head snapped forward, and he stiffened. The pounding in his head flared again, and wearing his helmet only intensified the pulsing pain, but he couldn't do anything about it.

"What were you looking at?"

Aeron's mind froze like it did when he'd first seen the blonde girl, only this time the reason sucked. He blurted the first thing that came to his mind. "Bugs, sir."

"'Bugs?' What in the third hell are you talking about, Ironglade?" Commander Brove glared at him.

"Bugs, sir," Aeron repeated. "They were flying around, and I—"

"If *bugs* concern you this much, you should remove yourself from our ranks," Commander Brove said. "If you somehow manage to bond with a wyvern—an unlikely prospect from what I've observed thus far—you'll have insect entrails coating your teeth by the end of your first flight."

Aeron couldn't tell whether or not Commander Brove was serious. The guy didn't seem like he even had a sense of humor, but his words elicited a few lackluster chuckles from the Featherwings around Aeron.

"Yes, sir," was Aeron's safest response, so he said it.

Commander Brove stared daggers at him for another long moment.

"Frankly, Ironglade, I'm surprised you made it to the courtyard at all, given your condition when I dragged your miserable corpse from your bunk this morning. But now you've got me curious: how did a useless sack of vomit like you get inducted into our ranks in the first place?"

Aeron's mind stalled again. *Why is he singling me out?*

He started, "I—"

"Answer loud enough for everyone to hear," Commander Brove barked.

Aeron wanted to lash out at him. Instead, he replied, "I excelled with the spear while serving in the cavalry, sir. I worked hard to earn a recommendation from Commander Engstrom, and he sent me along based on merit."

"Based on *merit?*" Commander Brove scoffed. "I wasn't aware that Commander Engstrom valued *idiocy* and *distractibility* as meritorious qualities."

"Commander Engstrom is an upright man and a model soldier," Aeron blurted. He'd had enough of Commander Brove's demeaning talk, and he certainly wouldn't tolerate any jabs at Commander Engstrom. "And I happen to believe he's an excellent judge of character."

"You've got quite the mouth on you, *recruit.*" Commander Brove approached Aeron with his hands behind his back, and he didn't stop until they stood face-to-face, their noses separated by only three inches of air.

Aeron could smell smoked meat on Commander Brove's breath, but Commander Brove had to be getting the worse end of that deal. Aeron's mouth still tasted like booze and a touch of vomit from the night before.

But Commander Brove didn't move. He continued to stand before Aeron, sturdy as a statue.

"I'm not interested in 'character,' Ironglade." Commander Brove's eyes narrowed. "I need men who can follow orders and men who can fight. Can you follow orders, Featherwing?"

"Yes, sir!" Aeron barked.

"Can you fight?"

"Yes, sir!"

Commander Brove gave him a wry smirk and stepped back. "Then prove it."

Aeron didn't move, uncertain. Fortunately, Commander Brove continued.

"Normally, these Featherwings would be sent away," Commander Brove addressed the recruits around Aeron. "But thanks to Featherwing Ironglade's audacity and Commander Engstrom being an 'excellent judge of character,' I'm feeling magnanimous."

Aeron gulped. Wherever this was going, it wasn't good. His headache agreed with him.

"As such, I've decided that three of the Featherwings who failed to make it to the courtyard in time will be eligible to return," Commander Brove began, "if they can prevail in combat against Featherwing Ironglade and each other."

Aeron shuddered. He didn't mind a good sparring session, but after the night he'd had, the lack of sleep that had followed, and the constant quaking in his head, he didn't feel like much of a combatant at the moment.

Without a command, the two Steelwings accompanying Commander Brove supplied a mass of wooden practice weapons from some nearby racks and barrels. They dumped the weapons in the center of the courtyard and then retreated to their posts near the tardy Featherwings, all of whom had perked up at Commander Brove's words.

Commander Brove picked up a staff with its tip scraped to a dull point.

"We'll host a battle royale of sorts. Last three standing get to stay." Commander Brove examined the staff in his hands. "And, of course, Featherwing Ironglade..."

Aeron braced himself for the inevitable bad news.

"That rule includes you. If you don't make it to the end, you're out."

Aeron's jaw tightened, and his head continued to hammer at him from the inside. But he couldn't focus on that now—not when he was about to fight to save his dying dream.

"But don't worry," Commander Brove taunted, "you were here on time, so you get an advantage: you get your weapon before the fight commences. Everyone else has to fend for themselves."

He tossed the spear to Aeron, who, despite his headache and his general malaise, caught it. Rings of wood a few inches behind the tip added additional weight to the end, making it comparable in weight to a real spear.

Great. What a huge help.

He held the spear at the ready, and all the disgraced Featherwings tensed, ready to spring forward.

Commander Brove glanced between them, stepped back, and said, "Begin."

A tidal wave of bodies flooded the center of the courtyard. Aeron estimated at least a dozen recruits had been late to the courtyard that morning, and they all crashed into the pile of weapons, grabbing for whatever they could snatch up first.

Sparring rules in the Govalian Army were simple: officers or another designated official monitoring the fight would determine if a blow from a practice weapon was fatal, and if it was, they called out the recipient of said blow. Then the fight would either restart or, in this case, conclude for whoever "died" in combat.

Aeron considered diving in and stabbing at his fellow Featherwings to knock a few out early, but he decided to stay out of the initial meat-grinder at the weapons pile. Better to let them thin themselves out first.

The two Steelwing officers circled the battle, scrutinizing the Featherwings and their fighting. Commander Brove stood in place, doing the same. They immediately called out three of the dozen or so soldiers, and the losers vacated the skirmish, heads hanging even lower than when they'd walked into the courtyard.

The remaining recruits scattered, now wielding weapons, except for two men in the middle who now fought over the lone remaining wooden dagger. Aeron didn't envy them. Although he was curious to see the outcome of their fight, he couldn't focus on it now.

As he'd expected, the majority of the Featherwings had fixed their attention on him. No doubt, they wanted to make a better impression, and what better way to do it than taking Aeron, the most recent focal point of Commander Brove's scorn, out of this competition?

Several of them rushed him, and the rest engaged each other. Wood clacked, and men and women grunted as they fought to keep their place in the corps.

Aeron was never more grateful that he'd trained with the spear than in that moment. As the recruits barreled toward him, most of them wielding wooden swords and axes, Aeron went to work.

His spear gave him a length advantage, which proved essential in dealing with so many foes. It bought him time to deal with them individually.

He feigned an attack at the nearest Featherwing's head. When the guy flinched and tried to parry with his sword, Aeron quickly redirected the tip of the wooden spear into his now-exposed breastplate. A dull *thunk* signaled the recruit's defeat, and the voice of one of the Steelwings confirmed it.

The second Featherwing closed in too quickly for Aeron to deliver another meaningful attack with his spear, and he was already swinging his sword at Aeron's head.

Instead of trying to block the blow, Aeron ducked under it and stepped past the Featherwing, and he whipped his spear around low and behind him. It struck the Featherwing in the back of his knee, and he went down.

Aeron would've finished him with a blow to the back of his head, but this was one of the guys who hadn't worn a helmet. He didn't actually want to hurt the guy, so he aimed lower and jammed the wooden spearhead into the center of his back instead. The recruit's armor ate the blow, and a Steelwing called him out.

"Careful, Ironglade," Commander Brove chided. "You almost left us there."

Aeron wanted to retort, but the next Featherwing didn't give him a chance. This one, a woman about Aeron's age and nearly just as large, also wielded a spear.

As they traded a few blows, Aeron could tell this wasn't her first choice for a weapon. She clearly hadn't trained with it much, and the infantry boots stamped on her breastplate told him she was probably accustomed to swords, the standard weapon for Govalian infantry.

He easily ducked under her next attack, planted the butt of his spear behind her ankle, and swept her feet out from under her. A quick jab to her sternum with the spear tip knocked her out of the competition. With a huff, she stood, tossed the spear to the ground, and left the courtyard.

Seven Featherwings remained, including Aeron. Seven Featherwings, but only three spots. Neither of the two men fighting for the last dagger had made it through, and the remaining recruits all stood with plenty of distance between each other.

Their zeal to take Aeron out specifically had faltered, and they now all eyed each other warily. Perhaps his performance thus far had dissuaded some of them, or perhaps they were just too focused on making it through that his involvement didn't matter anymore.

"If you all just stand there, I'll rescind my offer, and *none* of you will continue with wyvern knight training," Commander Brove threatened.

That got everyone moving. The biggest one came for Aeron with a roar, swinging an axe like he meant to chop Aeron in half, and faster than he'd expected. Aeron had no time to parry, so he raised his spear shaft to block the attack.

SNAP.

The wooden axe blasted through Aeron's spear, severing it in two pieces. Aeron staggered back, stunned. In all his time training, he'd never had a spear break during combat, whether in training or in an actual conflict. This guy was strong, and now Aeron's length advantage was gone.

As the axe-guy pulled back for another swing, Aeron noticed the spear left behind by the female Featherwing he'd defeated earlier. If he could somehow—

The axe lashed toward his head this time, and Aeron caught it with the two halves of his spear in an X-shape over his helmet. The axe stopped, but then the axe-guy kicked Aeron in his chest, sending him sprawling to his back.

Now he was even farther from that extra spear, and the harsh kick and ensuing landing sent fresh pain throbbing in his head.

As the axe-guy stalked closer, Aeron caught sight of Commander Brove's face. He was sneering.

It reminded Aeron of his father.

The sight, and the memories that accompanied it, filled Aeron with rage. He'd come this far. No matter what Commander Brove threw at him, no matter what stood in his way, Aeron would push through it. He had to.

I'm not a disgrace.

Now, he just had to prove it.

The axe-guy hefted the weapon over his head for a final blow, but Aeron rolled to the side, and the wooden axe blade clacked against the courtyard's stone floor. Then Aeron rolled back and stabbed at the axe-guy with the pointy end of his broken spear.

He hadn't expected to land a hit, and sure enough, the axe-guy pulled back just in time. But Aeron was ready for that.

As he sat up, he abandoned his weapons and grabbed the axe-guy behind his knees. He pushed up onto his feet, still low, drove his shoulder into the axe-guy at an angle, and he lifted. All those years working in Pa's blacksmith shop had made Aeron strong, too—strong enough, anyway.

Aeron dumped the axe-guy on his back, avoided a wild swing, and dove past him. He rolled forward, up to his feet and scrambled toward the extra spear. He snatched it up and whirled back in time to see the axe-guy make it back up to his feet.

The axe-guy started forward, only to get stabbed from behind by another Featherwing. He glanced back, stunned, and then spouted a deluge of curses, several of them aimed at Aeron, but most of them aimed at the guy who'd taken him out.

Now only four of them remained. The three other Featherwings all stalked toward Aeron at once. Apparently, they'd decided that the three of them would make it through at Aeron's expense.

He didn't know or recognize any of them, and he didn't know if they knew each other or not, either, but they'd clearly allied against him.

But he only needed to beat one of them. If he could take one out before the others got him, that was it.

An idea sprang to mind, and Aeron glanced back at Commander Brove. "You said that only three of us will make it through, right, sir?"

"Correct." Commander Brove's sneer had diminished some, but it was still there.

"Good."

Aeron wasn't a fan of abandoning his weapons in the middle of a battle, but given the terms of this conflict, he decided it was worth the risk. Plus, if this worked...

Rather than trying to fight three guys at once, he could end this now. He shifted his grip on the spear so he held it overhead, and he hurled it like a javelin at the guy in the center of the trio.

It caught him off-guard, and though he tried to evade it, he was too close for Aeron to miss, and the spear plunked against the center of his breastplate. The spear clattered to the courtyard floor.

He looked up at Aeron, then at the Steelwings, then at Commander Brove.

Commander Brove's sneer had shifted into a scowl. Instead of addressing the loser, he glared at Aeron. "Fall back in rank, Ironglade."

Aeron exhaled a relieved sigh, even though Commander Brove glowered at him with every step toward the ranks of Featherwings.

For now, all Aeron could do was try to ignore him.

Several Weeks Later

"You know the drill, Ironglade," said Brahm Ableman, one of the Leatherwings supervising the recruits. "Carry the water buckets up, bring the waste buckets down."

Aeron sighed and took the two heavy buckets from Brahm's hands. A bit of water sloshed over the edge and spattered on the floor, and he grunted.

At least I'll get another glance at the hatchery.

The male wyverns had fertilized the eggs right before the induction of Aeron's class of Featherwings, and while the incubation period varied with each litter, all the Leatherwings and higher-ranking officers kept insisting they could hatch "any day now."

Until then, for several hours every day, Aeron hauled water buckets from the well at the bottom of the fortress all the way up to the roost. While up there, he'd use the water for various tasks, most of which involved cleaning up after the wyverns, filling their water troughs, or refreshing the soldiers' latrines.

Aeron gazed up at the stairs leading up into the fortress until someone knocked into him from behind, and he staggered forward a step. More water sloshed out of the buckets, and Aeron mumbled a curse.

"Get moving, Ironglade." The voice belonged to Porgus Darleton, another Featherwing.

Aeron shot a glare back at him. Thus far, Porgus had prodded him at every available opportunity. Apparently, one of the recruits Aeron had defeated in Commander Brove's impromptu battle royale was a friend of Porgus's.

"You deaf from all that hammering as a kid?" Porgus taunted. He nudged another Featherwing next to him, who snickered. Like Aeron, both of them carried water buckets. "Never met a blacksmith with good hearing."

"And how many blacksmiths have you met, Porgus?" Aeron asked, unamused.

Porgus frowned. "That's not the point. Are you gonna move or not?"

Aeron ignored them and trudged up the stairs.

While in the cavalry, Aeron had seemed to be in relatively good shape, but climbing hundreds of stairs while burdened with so much extra weight, and doing so multiple times a day, made him rethink his assessment.

The majority of Aeron's "training" thus far hadn't focused on much of anything to do with becoming a wyvern knight or attaining a significant understanding of the majestic beasts. In addition to the water, he'd spent plenty of time shoveling mounds of wyvern manure and hauling buckets of it back down the stairs, too.

The first few times, he'd grown nauseated from the smell, but he only threw up once. After that, it didn't bother him as much anymore.

All the while, Aeron stayed optimistic. Once those eggs started hatching, Featherwings would become Leatherwings.

Minutes later, tired but not completely worn out, Aeron crested the top step and entered the roost. He'd lost a bit more water on the way up, but not enough to matter.

Porgus and his friends lagged farther behind, for which Aeron was grateful. He'd heard them muttering and whispering about him on the way up, and it was all he could do to keep himself from confronting them.

"Time to water the lizards," said the Leatherwing at the top. "Start at the first two stalls, and work your way around when you come back."

Aeron nodded.

Under the open ceiling, the roost looked and smelled the same as always. Wyvern stalls, each wide enough to accommodate a wyvern's twenty-foot wingspan and corresponding length, lined the walls around a large central platform—the launch pad.

Aeron poured his buckets into the nearest trough. A pair of wyverns from the two closest stalls chirped, lurched forward, and slurped up the water almost as fast as Aeron poured it in, sending a tremor snaking up Aeron's back.

Around them, other wyverns perked up, and their reptilian heads rose above their respective stalls as they, too, chirped and scanned the roost. Some also sniffed the air and chomped their mouths open and shut, a motion which Aeron had come to learn meant they were hungry.

Though chains restrained all the wyverns to their respective stalls, and though they'd never shown interest in snacking on him, Aeron still shuddered every time one of them charged forward, eager for a drink or some food.

They were huge beasts with long necks, enormous wings, and sharp teeth. If they'd wanted, they could easily rip Aeron apart. Fortunately, they'd acclimated to his presence, though part of him wondered if he'd still feel that primal fear of these incredible animals once he was bonded to one.

If he was able to bond to one. It wasn't a guarantee, though he tried to stay confident about his chances.

Porgus and his friends reached the top of the stairs with their usual clamor, giving Aeron an excuse to move on from the thirsty wyverns. He headed into the hatchery antechamber to his right for another look at the eggs.

With the number of torches burning inside the hatchery, the room was both well-lit and uncomfortably warm. Several table-like platforms, all of them made of stone and with their tops hollowed out, held a couple dozen eggs nestled within beds of straw.

The off-white eggshells glistened under the light and the heat, each slightly bigger than the largest watermelon Aeron had ever seen. A bit of color accented some of them, others had faint spots, and some were plain.

Aeron surveyed them with awe, and he couldn't help but smile. One of these eggs might hold his lifelong riding partner.

He didn't fully understand the bond between rider and wyvern, but the Leatherwings and officers had described it as an innate connection, almost as if a piece of the rider's soul belong to the wyvern, and vice-versa.

As he stared at the eggs, footsteps approached from behind him. He turned back, prepared to apologize for slacking or to defend himself from Porgus if need be, but neither proved to be the case.

Instead, the beautiful blonde girl with the pointed ears walked toward him.

She must've recognized the look of terror and confusion on Aeron's face, because she smiled and said, "We've been in the same training class for nearly two months now. Don't you think it's time you stopped staring and introduced yourself instead?"

Aeron gulped. He'd wanted to do exactly that ever since he'd first saw her, but he hadn't worked up the courage to do anything more than stare at her from a distance.

When he didn't say anything, she continued, "I'll start, then. I'm Faylen Uridi."

She extended her hand toward him. It gave him something else to awkwardly stare at, so he was grateful for the interruption.

He gulped again. Only when he took hold of her hand did he manage to make eye contact with her again.

"Aeron Ironglade," he managed to reply as they shook hands.

"Pretty incredible, aren't they?" Faylen let go of Aeron's hand and looked at the eggs.

Aeron still couldn't believe she was talking to him. He turned back for a look, standing next to Faylen. "Uh... yes. Definitely."

"I've heard all sorts of rumors about the bonding process after hatching," she said, her voice quieter, almost reverent.

"Like what?" Aeron asked.

"It can be instantaneous, or it can take several minutes. One Leatherwing told me he once saw a wyvern wait for more than an hour before it chose a rider."

"Whoa."

"Some claim that wyverns only bond with riders who are pure of heart," she continued, "but that can't be true. There are certainly bad wyvern riders out there, so there must be wyverns with affinity toward them, same as any other type of person."

"That makes sense," Aeron said.

He stood a head taller than her, and she looked up at him. "You're much more talkative around the other recruits and Commander Brove."

Aeron smirked. "I think the word you're looking for is 'mouthy.'"

Faylen smiled, and it send shudders through Aeron's body. The sensation matched the shock of terror Aeron felt whenever the thirsty wyverns launched toward him as he replenished their water supply.

"Do you think you'll bond with one?" she asked.

"I hope so." Aeron looked toward the eggs again.

"Porgus doesn't seem to think you will."

Aeron glanced at her, incredulous. "Porgus thinks that drinking from the wyverns' troughs will give him a better chance of bonding with one."

Faylen chuckled. "Seriously?"

Aeron nodded. "Saw him dunk his head right in and drink from them several times."

"That's disgusting."

"Yeah. Suffice it to say, I'm not too concerned about what he thinks."

She shook her head, still smiling. "Fair enough."

"You two," a voice called from behind them, and they turned back to see a Steelwing officer scrutinizing them. "What are you supposed to be doing right now?"

"Nice to finally chat with you, Aeron Ironglade." Faylen grinned. "Hope we can do it again sometime."

Aeron had no idea if she meant anything by it other than taking her words at face value, but he managed to reply, "Likewise."

She left him behind, and before he returned to his duties, he took one last look at the eggs within. The idea to drink from one of the wyvern troughs crossed his mind.

He considered it, then he shook his head. "Just... gross."

A Few Nights Later

"They're hatching!" someone shouted just as Aeron was trying to fall asleep.

The words charged through his body, burning in his veins and muscles as he sprang from his bunk and pulled on some daytime clothes, then his boots.

Along with a throng of other Featherwings, he rushed across the moonlit courtyard to the stairs leading up to the roost. His heart pounded from the exertion and the excitement of the moment, even as he tried to remain calm.

By the time he reached the roost, Aeron could barely breathe. Worse yet, he'd arrived among the middle of the pack, so most of the space inside the hatchery was already taken by other recruits, each of them just as hopeful as he was to pair with a newly hatched wyvern.

At nearly six feet, he wasn't short, but he wasn't tall enough to get a good view of the eggs, either, even standing on his toes. He did, however, see Faylen standing on the far side of the room. Her nearly white blonde hair was hard to miss.

Someone bumped into Aeron from behind, hard enough that it wasn't an accident. He grunted and turned back.

Porgus. Of course it was Porgus.

"What are you so excited about, Ironglade?" he hissed, far closer to Aeron than necessary. "You're just a blacksmith's son. You'll never bond with a wyvern. You might as well leave now."

Porgus's friends snickered behind him.

"Go drink some more wyvern water, Porgus." Aeron pinched his nose. "Might actually improve your breath."

Before Porgus could reply, a loud *crack* split the room, silencing the murmurs of everyone in attendance. A reptilian screech, high-pitched and weak, sounded next, followed by gasps from the Featherwings closer to the eggs.

"*Quiet*, everyone," ordered a sharp Urthian-accented voice. Aeron turned toward the source and found Commander Brove standing among the Featherwings, flanked by two Steelwings. All three of them wore their armor.

Aeron peered between the crowd, both trying to catch a glimpse of what was happening and trying to figure out if General Cadimus had joined them as well. He couldn't see anything of consequence, but in the end, it didn't matter.

Another chirp sounded, then the fluttering of wings, then a wet smack. More chirps, and then a gasp as one of the recruits was chosen. The bond was forged, apparently, in that instant, and the recruit held up a green-and-brown wyvern for all to see.

He cried, "Leatherwing!"

The recruits all clapped and cheered, Aeron included, until Commander Brove hushed them again.

"The first hatching is always the most exciting," he declared. "But trust that with each bonding, your sense of dread will increase. You will begin to wonder if you will ever be chosen, if you are worthy of bonding with one of these majestic creatures, if you have what it takes to become a Govalian Wyvern Knight.

"You are right to worry. You are right to fear the outcome of this night," he continued. "Most of you will not bond with a wyvern tonight... or ever. And if you fail to bond with one tonight, you will leave this roost for the last time, never to return. Ours is a sacred and noble—"

Crack.

Commander Brove stopped, and everyone fell silent again. Though Aeron still couldn't see, he knew what was happening. They all did. And sure enough, Aeron's anticipation now matched his fears of not bonding.

But even so, his hopes still burned. This was his future. It had to be, if for no other reason than he had nothing else.

The next egg hatched, and a wyvern spilled onto the floor with another wet splat and more screeching. A moment later, it found its recruit, and another Leatherwing was forged. This time, he received only modest clapping and a few half-hearted cheers.

A veteran Leatherwing led him and the first recruit out of the nest, through the sea of eager Featherwings, and Aeron got a good look at both wyverns when they went past. They were larger than he'd expected, each a little bigger than a large cat, but with wings and scales instead of fur.

Slimy, too.

What struck him most, though was the look in the newly minted Leatherwings' eyes. They almost literally glowed with joy. Aeron could only imagine what they were feeling inside.

Rather than continuing his sermon about the noble fraternity of the Wyvern Knight Corps, Commander Brove told everyone to shut up again as they waited for the next egg to hatch. They didn't have to wait long.

Another crack. Another wet smack. Another set of chirps, plus some cooing this time.

But instead of another random recruit, this wyvern chose Faylen.

Faylen squealed as she bent down to pick up her wyvern, out of Aeron's sight.

When she arose, an orange beast with purple stripes lay with its body coiled around the back of her neck, resting on her shoulders. Slime from its wings and torso darkened the fabric on her tunic, but she didn't seem to care.

She smiled, and Aeron smiled, too. He didn't know Faylen as well as he would've liked, but if it were up to him, she deserved to bond with a wyvern. Another veteran Leatherwing escorted her through the recruits, taking her and the wyvern elsewhere in the roost.

As she passed Aeron, she stopped and looked up at him. Her wyvern looked at him, too.

"This is Nilla." Faylen gave the wyvern some scratches under its scaly chin. Then she met his eyes again and said, "Yours is coming soon, Aeron."

It sounded like a promise, a certainty. She couldn't possibly know that for sure, but it renewed Aeron's hopes all the same.

He grinned at her. "Congratulations."

Nilla gave a squeak, then Faylen continued out of the hatchery.

As the night went on, they averaged a new hatching every ten minutes or so. The first two hours slipped by quickly enough, but everything after that seemed to drag on and on—except whenever a new hatching started. Then the Featherwings would perk up, watch closely, and wait for their next chance to be chosen.

"How do they all know to hatch at the same time?" Porgus muttered from behind Aeron.

If he were honest, Aeron was wondering the same thing, but he wasn't about to ask it aloud.

Another hour passed, then another. More wyverns hatched and bonded with recruits, more Featherwings became overjoyed Leatherwings, and more uncertainty crept into Aeron's heart.

Porgus's claims struck at him the hardest. *You're just a blacksmith's son. You'll never bond with a wyvern.*

The taunt echoed in Aeron's mind and resounded in his soul along with Commander Brove's taunts. He fought it all as best he could.

Still, he wondered, *What if the wyverns still in their eggs can sense my doubts?*

As more recruits bonded with wyverns, Aeron managed to get closer to the eggs. He ended up in the front row, shoulder to shoulder with other Featherwings, which also landed him under the bitter scrutiny of Commander Brove.

Between Commander Brove's persistent glares, Porgus's idiotic comments, and the ever-dwindling number of unhatched eggs, Aeron's confidence faltered even further.

At one time, he'd imagined bonding with a black wyvern, specifically. He could envision himself riding a dark airborne demon, laying waste to his foes with all manner of weaponry and attacks. Now he'd be thankful to bond with any wyvern of any color.

Another hatching led to another bonding. The recruit with his new wyvern turned to another Featherwing and said, "Wait 'til my pa hears about this!"

It shouldn't have hit him as hard as it had, but those words might as well have been a spear plunged into Aeron's gut. He felt sick, and then his own father's words added to the weight Aeron already carried from Porgus and Commander Brove.

"Some days—no, most days I wish I'd had a stronger, smarter son, but you're what I've got, so I'll have to make do." "Your sister will make a better blacksmith than you. If she were old enough, I'd replace you this very hour." "If you weren't so stupid, maybe you wouldn't constantly make bad choices." "You'll never amount to anything more than a blacksmith, so why bother dreaming of anything else?"

No matter how well Aeron thought he'd buried them, all the cruel things Pa ever said clawed their way to the surface of Aeron's memories.

He'd wanted nothing more than to prove Pa wrong, so he'd left home at sixteen and joined the Govalian Army instead of submitting to his father's will and living the rest of his life as a blacksmith. Becoming a Wyvern Knight would more than do the trick, but if he couldn't bond with any of the remaining wyverns...

As Aeron grappled with a lifetime of insecurities, another wyvern hatched—a brown beast with a tan underbelly and red eyes. It looked around for a minute while no one else dared to move.

Then, of all the recruits left, it chose Porgus.

He scooped it into his arms and showed it off to his two remaining friends who hadn't bonded yet, whooping and jeering. "I'm naming him Lash. We're gonna be friends forever, little guy. Wow... I can't believe this feeling..."

As a Leatherwing led Porgus and Lash out of the roost, the only feeling Aeron experienced was a deep emptiness in the pit of his stomach. Even Porgus had bonded with a wyvern.

"I *knew* drinking from the wyvern troughs would pay off!" he called back.

Despite it all, that stupid comment from Porgus actually made Aeron feel better, mostly because by that point he was absolutely certain that guzzling wyvern water had nothing to do with bonding.

Aeron's relief proved short-lived, however, when he realized his poor odds of bonding with a wyvern. By then, only six eggs remained, and well over twenty Featherwings still waited in the room, hoping against hope and believing for a miracle.

Commander Brove's expression had shifted from glaring to sneering at Aeron. Then he slowly shook his head, smirking.

The message was clear enough.

It's not over yet, Aeron tried to reassure himself. *I still have a shot.*

In thirty minutes, two more eggs hatched, and the wyverns bonded with their riders. A third hatched only five minutes later and chose a female recruit, only the second woman of the night to be chosen.

Three eggs remained. Aeron stared at them, refusing to look at anything else. He would *will* a bond into being. He couldn't do anything else but try to manifest it.

Another egg cracked. The wyvern's egg tooth pierced through, and chunks of the shell fell away. Aeron caught sight of a bluish green shimmer inside, and hope stirred within his chest.

Could it be...?

The wyvern spread its wings, still covered in slimy afterbirth from the egg's interior, and more of the egg cracked apart and toppled over. Only a small piece of the eggshell remained on top of the wyvern's head.

Gods... it's beautiful.

It was facing away from Aeron, searching the faces of the recruits opposite Aeron's position in the hatchery. Its head bobbed up and down, left and right, moving faster and faster, more frantically.

Aeron could almost feel the wyvern's fright and worry; he certainly felt plenty of tension himself. He stole a glance at Commander Brove, whose sneer persisted as he shook his head again.

I refuse to believe this is over, Aeron told himself. Then he focused and thought, *C'mon, little guy. I'm right here.*

The baby wyvern's head-bobbing stopped abruptly. He slowly turned his head back, and his body followed as he readjusted to get a look at the rest of the recruits.

As he did, Commandeer Brove's sneer melted into an expression of shock... or even horror. He shook his head again, but it wasn't the same as the last few times.

Aeron's heart pounded. Some of the past wyverns had taken up to a few minutes to find their riders, so he couldn't be sure how long this one would take to make its choice.

C'mon, wyvern. Choose me.

When the wyvern fully turned to face them, he locked his golden eyes on Aeron.

A rush of electric energy pulsed through Aeron, starting with a tingle in his nose. It shot down his neck, into his chest, arms, legs, fingers and toes.

The bond. It had to be.

Then the wyvern leaped off the table, and with two flaps of its newborn wings, it tackled Aeron to the floor.

It was absolutely disgusting. Slimy, bloody afterbirth clung to Aeron's face, chest, and arms as the wyvern wrapped its wings around Aeron's torso. When he realized the wyvern was hugging him—literally—Aeron's revulsion at the experience faded.

The bond replaced it, and Aeron changed forever.

He laughed, and the wyvern chirped and screeched with glee.

They were bonded. For life.

When Aeron finally managed to stand again, his wyvern still clung to him. Aeron met Commander Brove's eyes first and received nothing but a scowl.

It didn't bother Aeron in the least, and he grinned in return.

Leatherwing Brahm Ableman approached from among the crowd, also smiling. "Congratulations, *Leatherwing* Ironglade. If you'll follow me, please..."

Aeron complied. This was still so surreal, so impossible. He now understood the feeling Porgus had tried—and failed—to describe.

"Have you thought about what you're going to name it?" Brahm asked as they walked out of the hatchery.

Aeron hadn't given much thought to it. He supposed a powerful name would suit a wyvern, something to stoke fear and inspire respect.

But when he realized the wyvern still had that little piece of eggshell clinging to the top of his head, like a little white hat, Aeron reconsidered.

It looked like the wyvern was wearing a little wafer on his head.

Aeron plucked it off and dropped it behind them as they walked, then he smiled at Brahm. "Wafer. His name is Wafer."

Brahm just shrugged. "Wouldn't be my first choice, but he's your mount, Ironglade."

Aeron met Wafer's golden eyes again, and their bond renewed.

Then Wafer chomped his mouth open and closed several times, with several little *clop-clop-clops*.

Aeron didn't even have to ask. Through the bond, he knew what Wafer was saying.

"Uh... Brahm?" he said. "I think he's hungry."

CHRISTOPHER D. SCHMITZ
Award-Winning Multi-Genre Author

Author Christopher D. Schmitz

CHRISTOPHER D. SCHMITZ authors Sci-Fi, Fantasy, and Nonfiction books and has been published in both traditional and independent outlets. He has been featured on television broadcasts, podcasts, and runs a blog for indie authors . . . but you've probably never heard of him. Keep tabs on Chris by joining his mailing list. You can get free books and other updates by signing up for that list at: **www.AuthorChristopherDSchmitz.com.**

Chapter Two

Watch Of The Starsleepers

By: Christopher D. Schmitz

"THEY KILLED LENNY," DAVE hissed.

Barb stared at him blankly. "I don't understand why that bothers you," she said, injecting another egg with genetic material. "You know what every Watcher knows. We all have an expiration date. When the tribunal decides that..."

"No," Dave said. "This wasn't a 'forced expiration.' They *murdered* him."

Barb cocked her head. Murder was an archaic act that the cloned watcher race had nearly forgotten possible. Her face remained placid, though she'd also been Lenny's close friend. Watchers weren't supposed to form intimate bonds with their peers, knowing they would be culled at relatively premature ages. It was central to the watcher philosophy.

Dave sighed through his nose and let the silence envelop them. Only gently vibrations filled the air as the massive generation ship *Endymion* rocketed through space on its way to Alpha Centauri, Terra's closest neighbor. Technology allowed advances in space travel and the trip would take roughly one hundred and sixty years. They were currently in their eighth decade and Dave, watcher DAV-F, was the fifth iteration of the original clone, DAV-A.

Within a few days' time, a much younger LEN-F would take over Lenny's function in the fabrication shop. Dave pouted, "I'm not going to call him Lenny."

Barb raised a brow. "What will you call him, Lenph?" she annunciated.

Dave laid his head down on her workbench.

Barb reached down and squeezed his hand. "Listen, Dave. You know I love you, but these embryos aren't going to fertilize themselves. Who knows, one of these might be Len-G. Wouldn't that be ironic?"

He looked up at her. He did love Barb, but he knew she couldn't sympathize. Not really. Watchers didn't have the capacity, or so they were taught from the moment they were pulled from the incubation chambers and strapped into education implanters, a kind of mental download system that uploaded formative memories and base-level knowledge necessary to continue the role of the original genetic material.

Still, though, it felt a little comforting to hear Barb say she loved him. Watchers were allowed platonic relationships, but romantic entanglements were punished severely. A neurological device implanted at the base of the skull of each watcher mitigated sexual impulses, and provided negative correction when necessary. Dave laid his head back down on the table. He wished the device mitigated grief.

"Will there be a memorial?" Barb asked.

Dave forced himself back into an upright position. "Yes. There is always a memorial." He logged into the network and pulled up the Transition Schedule. The ship housed over twenty thousand watchers at any given time, so multiple transitions happened daily--that was when the new clone assumed the duties and life of his or her predecessor.

A thought solidified in Dave's mind: if Lenny was murdered, all evidence would disappear as soon as the F variant took over Lenny's life.

Dave stood. "I, uh, should go."

Barb shrugged, still preoccupied with her work. She still had several hours left of her shift and until then, she would remain distracted. Barb might have been warmer were it not for work--all watchers were conditioned to take their work seriously. The spinal devices, commonly called a "neuri," ensured it.

Dave and Lenny were as close as brothers, but Dave and Barb *might* have been *more...* in a world other than a cold clone ship hurtling through the void and where a death sentence hung over each creature.

He headed for the exit. It slid open as he approached.

"Hey," Barb called.

Dave turned.

"Tonight? Just you and me. We'll remember Lenny properly? We don't need some official ceremony, or to get LEN-F involved. I've just... work is important."

He nodded. Glad for the offer, and he could empathize. The neurological spine-chips often muddied thoughts of non-work-related tasks during scheduled shifts. "Tonight."

Dave held an old jar of cloudy liquid in one hand. He clutched Lenny's spare key in his other and took a swig of the mind numbing stuff watchers brewed in the engine bays. The Tribunal learned in the first generation that they couldn't program the neurological spine devices to punish alcohol consumption.

They'd tried, but that same punishment subroutine for alcohol affected watchers who used medication. They lost nearly all the A-generation watchers who refused to seek treatment for minor injuries as a result. Booze was forbidden, but consumption often went unpunished.

Right now, Dave and Barb didn't care about legalities. They were both hammered, and it was late. Order-keepers only patrolled sporadically.

"You're sure we won't wake Lenph?" Barb asked, louder than she meant.

Dave shook his head. "Until the Transition, he's still pulling duty on third shift."

Barb shrugged. That made sense. Young watchers were apprentices until they took over the lives and jobs of their genetic predecessors. Barb worked in the fertilization labs, and the embryos were grown and aged to optimum development for an individual. Typically, during their mid-teens, a body was awakened and programmed, but a fresh psyche could only handle so much downloading; new watchers were sent to live with the man or woman they would eventually replace. Every twenty to thirty years, the cycle renewed.

Dave unlocked the door and entered. He'd spent many nights on the ratty couch Lenny had claimed from a busted storage unit years ago. He plopped down and wondered how much longer he had until the Tribunal assigned him an apprentice of his own.

Barb sat next to him. "There's no pillow."

Dave raised a brow.

"Lenph normally sleeps on the couch. His pillow's gone... he's claimed the bedroom."

Dave's face darkened.

"You still think Lenny was killed?"

"I'm certain of it."

Barb cocked her head. Understanding denial was a part of grief. "But Lenny had an apprentice. We all knew his days were short."

Dave stood and began rifling through a box of Lenny's belongings, which the Tribunal's officers would soon come to claim. "I know that. But it's what makes it a perfect cover up. I'm telling you, Lenny would have told me if he'd been given his orders report for expiration."

Barb put her hands on his shoulders and tried to comfort him. Dave turned. Their faces were so close their noses could have touched and a surge of endorphins rushed through them both. Dave nearly leaned in to kiss her; the alcohol made him throw caution to the wind.

A jarring bolt of pain seared through his mind like an icy spade. Barb felt it too, and they pinched the bridges of their noses to try to quell the agony caused by the neuri implanted at the base of the skull.

They each took a swig of the flammable, almost clear fluid. "I--I should go," said Barb, whose neck had remained flush since the jolt. She left before Dave could object.

He sat back on the couch with a box containing all that remained of his best friend and sifted through it. Dave scratched at the neuri on his spine and muttered, "I know they say these things keep us alive. But dammit, they itch."

Dave pulled out a recording device. They were often used to capture video of important data watchers needed to pass to their duplicates. This one had been hidden within a bolt of fiber batting.

Suspicion tore through Dave. If he'd known his expiration appointment, he'd have made a recording for Lenph and left it somewhere obvious. "It *was* a murder," Dave whispered, suspecting Lenny had stashed it somewhere safe so his friends could find it if tragedy struck.

Dave stared at the device for a long moment. He recalled an old rumor that the Tribunal had recording devices in barracks rooms. The AI supposedly didn't understand images well, but because it had the voice prints of every watcher on file, it could easily parse language. Dave had no idea what might be in the unit's memory bank. But if Lenny truly had been killed, he'd need to listen in a private place.

The chrono read that the hour was still late, or early, depending on your schedule. He dumped the device into a pocket and left.

Dave meandered the seldom used service corridors where lighting was sparse. He wedged his way into a hidden nook and retrieved the memo device. With the volume set low, he thumbed it active.

Lenny's recorded visage shone in a blur of holographic light. He was in his washroom; the vent fan rattled, and the handwash flowed. Anything that offered background noise to mask his words did, and it made his voice scratchy.

"Listen. They are coming for me. My ident-tag is LEN-E. I have not been given an expiration date yet, but the Tribunal will send a termination team for me, I am sure." Lenny looked up as if he heard something in the distance.

He returned to the recorder with panic on his face. "I was called to repair a system's malfunction in the bow. *Yes*, the *bow*, where watchers aren't allowed to go--I saw something in there--something terrifying. You wouldn't believe me if I told you... they're keeping it a secret. It's all a lie."

A loud thump penetrated the white noise at the sink. "Search for yourself. My team included ASA-D, BEN-G, and DAN-E."

Another thump. Lenny wrapped the recorder in the material, which crinkled as he stowed it in secret. It still picked up audio and the sounds of a struggle as the Tribunal's reclamation team dragged him away. Only the sound of the handwash remained.

Dave swallowed the sticky dryness in his throat and scanned the net for the names of Lenny's three coworkers. All were listed on the transition schedule. *Dead.* Two of them had asterisks by their name to indicate accidental death and rapidly aged clone replacements. RA-clones tended to be less stable. The process included extensive mental downloading in lieu of an apprenticeship; it made the mind brittle and tended to make watchers who burned out quickly under the stress of their jobs.

His body had filtered most of the alcohol out by now. The only lingering effect was the remaining courage enough to try something risky.

The bow. That was where they were. The humans. Endymion's *precious cargo. No watcher was allowed into the bow without special orders. Apparently, such assignments also earned a termination order.*

In the service hall, Dave was mostly hidden. A maintenance shaft lay at a nearby dead-end. He removed an access panel and slipped inside, cursing to himself as he went. The liquid courage remained, but his brain argued with the lingering chemical bravery.

Dave scurried through a tunnel with the low ceilings where tubes, piping, and cables hung. He scrambled, guided by the few runway LEDs. Luckily, if any work crews were assigned to duties in the corridor, he would see their lamps long before they ever spotted unauthorized watchers in the shafts.

After winding his way through the maze of connections, Dave arrived at a larger hall with a rounded aperture that was built into the bulkhead. A large warning was posted. *Forbidden Entry: punishable by death.*

The Tribunal did not mess around, Dave knew. Built into the door was a simple laser grid that sent an invisible signal to any neuri that passed through it. That trigger would overload the pain sensors of an unauthorized person and literally fry his or her brain with sensory overload.

His duties included routine power maintenance, and he knew that there was a scheduled outage connected to this region's grid. It would last several cycles... but important systems had backups. *How important to humans is killing inquisitive watchers?*

Dave sucked in his breath, held it, and then walked through the opening. Only after he confirmed he still lived did Dave relax.

He stole down the corridor and searched for an access port to the storage bay, but there didn't seem to be any. Dave muttered beneath his breath. He hadn't come all this way, only to be denied now.

A ventilation grid was mounted to the nearby wall. Dave examined it, but there were no bolts or any way to remove it. But he felt certain he could force his way through. As long as he did his best not to damage it, *or himself,* he thought, he'd get away with spying.

Dave charged at the panel and rammed his shoulder into it. And then found himself falling, tumbling into the dark.

Dave flailed through the air during a free-fall. And then he hit bottom, landing on his back so hard that he thought he heard vertebrae break in his neck. Something felt hot and sticky at his clavicle and reached behind as ground lights glowed softly in response to motion in the cavernous storage zone.

Checking his hand, he didn't find the expected blood, rather a trickle of fluid leaked from his neuri. Dave's heart plunged into his gut. *I'm going to die...* he paused, understanding he'd already risked death once and emerged fine. A few seconds later he realized that an early lesson ingrained upon watchers, *the neuri keeps you alive*, was a lie.

What else is false? He wondered, thinking to test if the device on his neck still functioned. Dave closed his eyes and thought of Barb. He liked Barb, *more than platonically*, and imagined her naked. Watchers were not permitted to see the opposite gender nude, so he wondered what it looked like. He used his imagination. His mind pounded with chemical excitement and his pants stretched with a rush of blood.

Pulse racing, Dave's eyes opened wide. He'd never experienced that before. Neuris staved off aspects of full sexual maturity. Dave poked his crotch and nearly doubled over at the new and sudden sensation.

He looked up. What his eyes saw was powerful enough to shut down even his newly raging sex drive. *Humans. Millions of humans.*

Dimly lit tubes of frozen analog gel revealed the floating forms of the precious cargo who were packed for more than a century of transit. Rows of clustered tech were stacked tall and stretched as far as Dave could see. His breath caught in his throat and he approached the nearest cryo unit, which kept a nude passenger in suspended animation.

The human hung in the viscous fluid with electronic leads monitoring the person's vital statistics. An organic mesh kept jaw and lips closed while a thin nose tube looped around the head, ready to provide air once the cryo tube activated its flash-thaw cycle which would make each pod reach 37C, standard body temperature, in less than one second after arrival at Alpha Centauri.

Dave looked left and right and made a startling realization. *DAV-E was human.*

He touched the glass and pulled his hand away, leaving a frosty print. He gasped, and no longer wondered what female anatomy looked like.

Dave touched the neuri at the back of his neck. He knew he was a clone. All watchers were reproductions, but they were all also human. For generations, watchers speculated what humans really were. Maybe they had tails, or scales, or multiple heads and communicated telepathically. But the rows of bodies in stasis revealed the truth. "I--I'm human? We're all of us... human?"

He grabbed at Lenny's recording tool and cleared space in the memory while still preserving his friend's last moments. Dave knew he had to record this, to take the evidence back to the other watchers. He corrected his own thoughts *to the other people*.

"Lenny's death will not have been for nothing."

Dave walked confidently through the laser grid, certain that a trigger for his neuri couldn't kill him, even if the power had been reactivated. Still half in shock, he returned to his quarters. Standing in front of the mirror in his lavatory, Dave stared into his own face. He found a spark in his eyes--something he could not articulate.

Something triggered inside him, as if a creature awakened. *Hope? Wonder?* He knew what humans were now. At least what they looked like. He had to share that... but he also needed a plan.

Lenny and others died because of that discovery, and the Tribunal would not allow to leak out easily. Dave grabbed a multi-tool, which he often used for hardware repairs. His primary watcher functions were in software applications, but he was often called to make physical repairs on the fly, and he was fairly adept at it.

Dave departed for the workshop area, where he sometimes had to fabricate special equipment for jobs. He gathered several items and soldered, wired, and screwed together a custom device for his own protection. A simple relay which would send a signal if he depressed the button.

No watchers gave him a second look while he worked. Dave often worked there, and none knew he was outside his shift.

He looked up when he spotted motion. A watcher near the door pointed directly at him, obviously speaking with someone beyond the threshold. And then a line of Order-Keepers dressed in black garb entered the room. They moved single-file and wore masks to conceal their faces. These were the watchers called into service if a clone failed to report for Transition. They were the ones who would have dragged away and killed Lenny.

Dave hadn't completed the failsafe device. He had not acted quickly enough. His heart sank, and he walked a line towards the executioners. Running would be futile, but at least he could walk to his death holding his head high and with human nobility.

The Order-Keepers jogged towards him, and then moved past, heading for a workstation in the tech bay. *Lenny's station.*

Adrenaline surged through Dave, making him feel electric. His neuri would usually mitigate its flow and dampen its effects. But not now. With pulse racing, he did his best to control his breathing and act normal. Dave left the bay and entered his regular workstation, passing by his coworkers and exchanging mundane nods of recognition.

He sat at his kiosk but did not activate the terminal. JAQ-F, Jack, sat at a nearby cubicle engrossed in his work. Jack stood and excused himself for a break. Dave slid around and into the adjacent berth as soon as the coast was clear. He quickly wrote a piece of code, a simple power interrupt he could use if needed. He'd only need to punch the toggle on the custom hardware he'd just made. Plugging the device into the data port via standard interface, he downloaded the software, unplugged it, and then deleted the software.

With any luck, there would be no detection. If the Tribunal's oversight and accountability software picked up what Dave had done, Jack might get a visit from the Tribunal's inquisitors.

Dave left his workplace and headed out. A twinge of guilt nagged at him. What if the Tribunal killed Jack? Jack was pretentious and unfriendly, but should neglecting to log off a terminal result in early termination? Is that human justice?

Before leaving, Dave watched as the Order-Keepers departed with a box of Lenny's things. They probably meant to destroy them and ensure no trace of the secret was left behind.

Dave turned the corner. "Yes," he announced. Humans *would* do that. They'd enslaved whole generations of their direct genetic descendants, denied them the full capacity of their bodies, and treated them as property--growing them and exterminating them at their own leisure. "Killing is a *very* human practice."

The fertilization lab was mostly empty by the time Dave arrived; it was this shift's lunchtime, Dave realized as he checked the chrono. He stared at it incredulously. Time had blazed by without much notice. But he assumed Barb was still there. She often ate lunch while remaining at her post in order to ensure nothing went wrong. Her work was critical.

Barb had once remarked her training taught her they had a finite amount of egg cells and so caution had to be taken when creating new the embryonic watchers. If they ran out of clones before *Endymion* arrived at Alpha Centauri, all could be lost. Barb had noticed that, for some unexplained reason, the supply counts of material never decreased and her team had been fertilizing cells for years.

She'd assumed there was an accounting glitch. Dave now knew better. *Watchers were human.* And before their remains were submerged into an amino pool to break it down into raw protein strings and remade into materials for watchers' consumption, the reproductive materials were likely harvested and stored for later use.

Dave entered the lab without sterilizing first.

Barb shouted at him. "You can't just barge in here without..."

"I was right. Lenny was murdered," he blurted out. Dave regretted it immediately. Unlike Lenny, he hadn't masked his words with white noise. It might be heard by the Tribunal.

"What are you talking about?"

Dave pulled out the recording device and held it up.

Barb asked, "What's that?"

He put a finger over his lips. "I can show you. But I need to know if you trust me?"

"What? Of course I..."

"Turn around and close your eyes. I'll help you see. Keep your eyes closed."

Barb did as instructed, though confused. "What are you going to show me?"

"I'll show you *everything.*"

Barb yelled as a jolt of pain rippled through her spine. Dave had rammed the sharp part of his multi-tool into her neuri's battery compartment and the implement pierced too far, pinching her flesh as it disabled the device. She whirled on him. "What are you..."

She stared at him with new eyes.

Dave touched his head to hers and Barb smelled him. Her brain reacted to the suddenly opened door and chemicals designed for procreation slammed into her like tidal forces washing over desert dunes. Pheromones nearly overcame her, and she clung to him, kissing him for the first time. Her mind swam with new impulses; Barb's body craved his.

"I have to tell you something," Dave said, pushing her away enough to look into her eyes. "Barb, *you are a human*. We both are."

"What are you talking about?"

"Damn it," he realized he'd run his mouth again in a sensitive area. "Come with me." Dave led her by the hand into a darkened corridor and played Lenny's recording, and then the one he took of the humans.

Barb could scarcely believe it. "I thought they'd have fur." The mental shock had quelled most of the chemical lust pounding through her body. Then she blanched. "Do you think the Tribunal knows that we know?"

Dave kept his lips tight and nodded resolutely. "I should have waited to tell you until we were away." He held her hand as they walked back towards the watchers' sector.

"What will we do, then?" Barb asked.

"I'm forming a plan," he flashed her a roguish grin.

They'd just cleared the service hall when they spotted Order-Keepers behind them. They projected an image of Dave and Barb as they asked a random passerby. That man pointed to the hall where they stood.

Dave nearly yanked her arm off as he dragged her behind. "Run!"

Dave and Barb scurried through the maintenance shaft ahead of their pursuit. Right now, the safest place for them was the humans' chamber. He did not know if the Tribunal's team could access it without earning a death sentence. Dave guessed they might be exempt. Right now, running was their only chance.

Barb skidded to a halt before the laser gate. Fear rooted her in place and she did refused to pass through. They were programmed early for obedience. "I--I'll die."

"No, you won't," Dave insisted, stepping through. "I disabled your neuri. They can't do anything to you. *You're a human*. This only kills watchers."

Barb squeezed her eyes and shuddered as she stepped through. She emerged unharmed, and the duo ran down the hall. They could hear the enemy far behind them requesting emergency override on the laser gate so they could pass.

Dave stopped at the aperture where he'd fallen once before. "It's a long way down. It might hurt. Leap of faith," he warned Barb and then plunged through.

This time, he landed in a half crouch and rolled to break his fall. The lights came up shortly afterward and Barb jumped. She fared better than him, able to judge the distance.

Barb stood and gasped when she saw the rows and rows of sleepers. "There are millions of them." She read the name plate on the base of one tube. "Aliyah Amber Jacobson. AAJ-0"

Dave took her hand. "There are millions *of us*. I suspect that each sleeper here has a genetic duplicate in the watcher pool."

A voice called out behind them and from above. "Stop there, or we'll shoot." The kill squad had been armed with lethal weapons.

Dave withdrew his device with the singular button and held it aloft. "*You* stop, or I'll push this button and kill every human in these pods!"

Their pursuers scoffed momentarily and then paused, cocking their heads, receiving orders via ear-piece. They retreated a few steps, keeping barely visible through the vent.

The new humans slipped behind a cluster of cryotubes, taking cover from the assassins' weapons. A speaker system activated with garbled words. "Parley."

Dave cocked his head. "Who is this?" His neck flushed and Dave realized he was well beyond any ability to form a new plan. He thought he and Babe could escape through the cryozone, but what then? The executioners would never stop.

"I am the Tribunal," the voice replied. "You have proved a resourceful and clever watcher, DAV-F."

Dave waved his device threateningly. "I am a human!" he yelled. "And if you wish to barter for the lives of the humans in stasis--the *precious cargo* you've enslaved generations of us for--then I want to talk in person."

"Very well."

Except for the millions of status LEDs on the tubes, all the lights went out. A runner of lumen strips created a path. They followed, and it led to a terminal in the center of the storage area.

Barb sucked in her breath, arriving in the heart of *Endymion*. Its mission was centered on this very spot.

Dave heard distant footsteps and guessed their pursuers had entered the compartment. He turned a circle. "Show yourself, Tribunal."

A light pulsed on a mechanical unit as the speaker sounded. The interface screen lit with a cascade of pixels forming a digital imitation of a face. "You are no more human than I, DAV-F... I am the Tribunal."

Footsteps clomped in the dark as the executioners surrounded Dave and Barb. She clung to him and Dave breathed her in her scent; it threatened to fog his brain with desire. He shook his head to clear it.

"Call them off, Tribunal," Dave insisted, waving his device. He suspected the computer program knew what he'd programmed it for.

"Stand down," ordered Tribunal.

Dave stared at the computer array. He guessed it's AI more clever than any human or watcher. "And tell them to throw their earpieces into the light." He didn't want Tribunal issuing orders privately.

The communicators clattered to the steel grid floor around his feet.

A plan finally formed in his mind. "I'd feel more comfortable with a gun, too," Dave insisted.

"Boss?" a voice asked in the dark.

"DAV-F claims to be human," Tribunal said, limited to his speaker. "Humans are rational creatures. DAV-F and I will resolve this with words and logic. A gun's presence will prove irrelevant. There is no fear... not if DAV-F is human."

A gun skittered towards him and Dave picked it up and bartered. "What will you offer this human to stand down?"

"You are not human."

"*I am* a human! My genetic blueprint proves it," Dave roared. "I think. I have feelings."

"Your logic is flawed. Humanity is not bestowed by acts of procreation: Tribunal was created by humans. Sentience cannot be its definition: Tribunal is fully sentient. I am not human."

Dave narrowed his eyes at the thing. It was connected to the ship, but housed within circuitry and drives. A mechanical brain in a box. "You are a created personality?"

"Yes. I am fully aware. But *I am not a human.*"

"Then what makes someone human," he demanded, "if it's not what we were born to be, what we do, or proved by self-awareness?"

A pregnant silence hung in the dimness. "Only humans decide what makes life human."

Dave thought back to that moment in the mirror. He'd recognized a spark within himself, and he rejected Tribunal's definition.

The speaker crackled. "Here is what I can offer: on humanity's behalf, I can *make* you human. Place you both in a pod for..."

Dave snapped the weapon to bear and unloaded the full magazine into Tribunal, slagging his housing and destroying him utterly. He whirled in time to see the executioners try to come to the controller's aid. Dave slapped the button on his wireless device.

A shrill warning tone filled the compartment, and the LEDs switched to red as the power to all the cryotubes' life support tripped off. Within seconds, millions passed away in their sleep.

The watchers stopped short of tackling Dave. "H-how could you?" The Order-Keepers stared at the darkened pods, minds obliterated by the lengths of Dave's bloodless carnage. "You murdered them all."

Dave retrieved the multi-tool from his pocket and stared at the first executioner's neuri. "But that's what proves we are human. Humans kill."

Using the tool, he freed his would-be assassins and took Barb's hand. "The things in these tubes weren't human anyway," Dave muttered. "If Tribunal was to be believed, then these things were monsters."

Watch of the Starsleepers won the **Silver Honorable Mention in the Writers of the Future Contest**. It was published in the 2022 collection, *Space Opera Digest: Have Ship Will Travel*

DARBY HARN

Critically Acclaimed Fiction Author

Author Darby Harn

DARBY HARN is the author of *Stargun Messenger*, an SPSFC Quarterfinalist, and *Ever The Hero*, which *Publisher's Weekly* called "an entertaining debut (that) uses superpowers as a metaphor to delve into class politics in an alternate America." His fiction appears in *Strange Horizons*, *Interzone*, and elsewhere. Learn more at: **darbyharn.com/**

Chapter Three
Every New Year's Eve In What Cheer, Ranked

By: Darby Harn

FIVE - Dive Bar On Main Street, 1972

U SUALLY, WHAT CHEER IS frozen solid in the dead of winter. After a few quarter cans of Schlitz, I was just going to walk out into the snow as far as I could. This particular New Year's, it rains, just pours down buckets and you come into the bar, soaked in a dress ticking with hundreds of tiny clock hands.

"What do you think?" you say. "Too much?"

Proper time travel etiquette discourages small talk, as this can be disruptive to the local timeflow. Even minor disruptions can create ripple effects that eventually shred all of reality to ribbons, so mostly you just observe. It's hard not to notice you, barefoot in a bar with colors painted in your hair.

You sit beside me at the bar. "Why so down?"

Though the time leap device I wore registered you as a red blip among all the blues, the rules forbade even acknowledging each other beyond a wink and a nod.

"We're supposed to blend in," I say.

You raise your glass at the three women at the far end of the bar, all dressed in the same era-appropriate pastel-colored polyester suit. Normally the Bureau of Temporal Integrity focuses on the obvious waypoints in time. Dawn of Man. Sinking of Atlantis. Elvis dying on a toilet. There's nothing here in cold, empty middle-to-late Iowa we can really change, except our own trajectories.

"So they notice me," you say. "I become a myth or legend or I get confused with The Ninth Incarnation of the Algorithm Ascendant. At least they get a story out of it."

"Those aren't just any women, you know."

You smile. "None of us are."

I try to focus on something else. The first *New Year's Rockin' Eve* plays on the TV. Christmas lights strand the bar. Cigarette smoke clouds the hanging glass lampshades over the pool tables. "Rocketman" plays on the jukebox and I'd be lying if I said I haven't taken some inspiration in my choice of footwear from Elton John. Otherwise, my attire functions entirely to defray attention: red polyester pants. White-checkered shirt. You can't be yourself, in time.

RULES OF TIME TRAVEL:

1. *Adhere to the moment.*

2. *Don't flaunt your temporally fluid lifestyle.*

3. *You break it, you buy it.*

Don't be fluid. Don't obstruct the flow. Makes sense.

It takes three more cans of Schlitz for me to say anything else. Not so much because of the women. They're redundant, as all bureaucracies are. I have my own monitor, in my head, snaked around my heart, choking every word. Sometimes I don't know what I even want to say, but I sit with a total stranger at the bar, talking, drinking, telling you about my fatigue with history and wearing these clothes that aren't my clothes and being this shadow of other people's lives just to squeak by with my own.

"I'm tired," I say.

You take my hand. "I know."

I order another beer. "You're braver than I am."

"What you do takes a lot more courage."

"What do I do?"

Your dress ticks toward midnight. "Fight yourself. Every second of every day."

"Why are you here? Tonight?"

"Listening. I never did that before."

"Listening?"

"Promise me. You'll keep going until you see me."

"See you when?"

The ball drops. Everyone blows their kazoos and hug and kiss, but you're gone. I run out in the rain, looking for you, but I don't have anything of yours, not a name or a shoe.

FOUR - The Forsyth Prescription Drug Store, 1879

I try dozens of New Year's. Hundreds. None of them fit. I can't find you in any of them and maybe you were just one of those glitches in the system. History is a program, running over and over, without deviation but every once in a while, you get a blip. A ghost image. A flaw in the code.

So I go back.

Farther into nowhere I sought before. On New Year's in 1879, What Cheer isn't quite nowhere anymore. The Burlington, Cedar Rapids, and Northern Railway has just built its line through the town. Local legend has it that a Scot named Robert Forsyth proclaimed *'What cheer with you!'* upon discovering the coal mine that granted him his fortune. I could dispel the myth easily enough, but it's not the past I want to clarify.

The clerk in the drug store hands me a pair of bottles of laudanum. "This is the quality article," she says, with a quaint earnestness. "We're the most careful of druggists."

I pocket the bottles in my sack coat. "Much obliged."

Outside, people line up just to get a look at you. Coal black hair. Dress pressed from charcoal tablet tins. No shoes, again, in the mud and snow of what will become Main Street.

You wink at me. "Warmer?"

That internal censor wrestles my tongue. What would I say, anyway? What did I want to tell you before, or have you understand? I don't understand. I wanted to hurt myself and then I wanted to find you and now you're here, and I'm heavy with medicine. But when I talked to you, the knots in me loosened.

I made sense.

I live in all these eras, and all these worlds, and I am all these people I write about, their habits and foibles and strange words. Never myself.

I take off my bowler hat. "I've been looking for you. I've searched for you through years and years. Centuries. I've been back to 1972 dozens of times."

"Oh, we're only there the once."

"How can you know that?"

"History comes with instructions," you say. "Not that you have to follow them."

"Do you know how this ends?"

You tap the bottles fat in my coat pocket. "Do you?"

"I'm tired," I say.

"From looking for me?"

My tongue grows as heavy as the bottles of laudanum, pulling the collar of my coat into the back of my neck, a noose scratching against my skin as I squirm on the block.

All your tin rattles as you shrug. "I never know what to say, either."

"You don't seem to have a problem getting it out."

"I just follow my gut. I say the bad things, so I only think good things. Mostly I think about women. All the time. Their hair. Their smell. Their clothes. Their shoes!"

I shake my head. "But you don't wear shoes."

"Well, I have to leave myself something to think about."

What do I think about? Women. All the time. Their hair. Smell. Clothes. Shoes. Sometimes I'm attracted to a woman, but it's not sexual. Like now. I don't know what this is. A closeness. A connection, beyond anything I've known before. A resonance.

Three women dressed in short fur jackets come down Main Street, toward the Opera House. All at once, they glance at us, as if they're all operated by the same root command.

You hook your arm in mine. "I forgot how scratchy the fabric of this suit was."

I try to stay out of the mud. "Have you been here before?"

"Only the once."

"What's your name?"

"That's against the rules," you say.

"Now you care about rules?"

Gunfire signals an early start to the festivities. Coal clouds and engine steam haze like the cigarette smoke in the bar in 1972. Your eyes grow distant, searching for something far off in the gloam.

"Their lives are so brief," you say. "So certain. More than half the men in this town will work in those mines. It's a great opportunity for them. The only one. This is all they'll ever be."

"What else could they have done?"

You look at me. "They're bound in circumstance, but all their toil and work broke our chains. Until time travel, every human life was compressed between the pages of a history book. No shape. No form. No question. Someone tore all the pages out of the book. We're the words, sliding off the page. Falling letters. We get to arrange them, however we wish."

Possibility defines my life. All my letters pile around me, burying me beneath my own expression. Divers go into the sea, to study sharks. They do it from inside a cage. That's time travel. That's been my life, and I don't know why it's not yours.

The women linger outside the opera house, pretending to chitchat, always keeping their eyes on us. Candles burn in the windows, and piano music plays inside, to laughter.

I guide us toward the saloon. "We have to be careful."

"History is bureaucracy," you say. "Always claiming to be for the benefit of tomorrow, but always fighting for the preservation of now. There is no now. There never has been."

"Isn't that all there is?"

"Right now, people have to light candles and kerosene lamps, just like they have for hundreds of years, but right now, tonight, in Menlo Park, Edison lights the first bulb."

"I've been there," I say.

"Things get brighter. But you have to want to live in the light." You glance at the women. "And not in the shadows."

"Light casts shadows."

"You only know the truth of something from its shadow."

"I can't just break the rules."

You shrug. "You don't have to live this kind of life. You don't have to find the most remote, unhistorical place in history to feel like you're not caving in all the time."

Somehow you know how I feel, without me having to say it. In the dive bar, in the muddy tract that would become Main Street, I'm less than incognito. I'm invisible.

Transparent.

You take my hat and put it back on my head. "Doesn't really suit you. None of this does. But the great thing about history is that it's mostly the future. And mostly unwritten."

I want to scream. "Why are you here?"

"I told you. To listen. What do you want to say?"

The sack coat itches my skin. I forget where I got it. Some other excursion into the 19th century. Time travelers never get clothes tailor-made, or tailor-fit. A modern hand betrays the artifice in what I am doing. The lie I am living.

My hand traces the tin curve of your dress. "I want to be like you."

You smile. "Want to try it on?"

THREE - The Last Ice Age, Circa 12,000 BC

This New Year's is more typical for Iowa. You still aren't wearing shoes. Never bothers you. Nothing bothers you. Not the mammoths or musk oxen, or the strange whistle in the air of the wind knifing through calving glaciers. To the east, the southern extent of the Wisconsinan Ice Sheet forms a pearlescent sheen across the horizon, as if the sky were sediment and the ice a layer of diamond buried deep at the bottom. Pressure forces me to hold my tongue, again. To hold myself back.

"I thought we were making progress," you say.

I hold myself against the cold. "You don't understand."

You pluck a pink flower off your dress. "I understand. Better than anyone."

Every word you speak is like warm air, sneaking into the crevices of the cracking ice sheet. The gap opens wider each day.

"How?" I say.

You tuck the flower behind my ear. "This place has been under ice for thousands of years, but it's going to be a garden. That garden is going to become a desert, eventually. But just because it happened, doesn't mean it will. That's why they're watching us, always."

Three dire wolves gray out of the snow. They watch us from a distance, but they won't keep it. Not this time.

"You should go," I say.

Your toes wiggle in the snow. "If I leave, the future may only be what is written. History isn't watching something play out to script. It's listening. Hearing the tones. The parts of the song you didn't that first time. Ever do that? Listen to a song a thousand times, and then one day, there's this bit of guitar. Or harmony. And the song is never the same."

Soft petals caress my cheek. "You're always different."

She plucks off another flower and sets it behind her ear. "Now we're the same."

"I want to be different. I want to be me." My shoes press overlapping tracks in the snow. "It's confusing."

"I spent too much of my life listening to doubt and fear. I didn't listen to myself. I always said, if I could go back anywhere, any time, I'd listen to me."

"But you know who you are," I say.

"Yes."

"Why do you come? Why are you so nice to me?"

"Because I know who you are."

The wolves close in.

I stand. "You should go."

"Do you still want to die?"

A sound like thunder cracks across the plain. The warming that melts this glacier and scars the land here in fertility can't be stopped now. In time, all this will be new.

"I'm messing up all my tenses," I say.

You plant one of your pink flowers in the soft ground, beneath the melting snow. "History is an illusion. The future doesn't exist. There's only today. Right now."

The wolves close in on us. Inevitability does. They take you. Leave me. Not one word passes between any of us, and words aren't necessary. I know what's happening now. After time travel, jails aren't necessary. Infinity denies the illusion of confinement, but there are limits to time. Petals of pink flowers drift across the snow. The world cracks.

Everything has its limit.

TWO - The Time That Time Collapsed

Time collapses on what would have been New Year's Eve in What Cheer if there were still a Gregorian calendar or people. There is not much of Iowa, either, though with some forensic analysis, I'm reasonably sure you can identify the chunks of molten earth that it had been.

You wear a kind of tuxedo, smart and chic and decidedly not prison attire, though that's what you are. BTI condemns problem cases here, in the slow melt of time. Time slows as it disintegrates, a bullet wobbling broadside, losing its momentum. Atomic reactions stop. Stars become slurry. Things like gravity and earrings and people break up into their component pieces.

I bring a bottle of the 1947 Cheval Blanc. May as well go out in style. "This is the end."

You pour us both a glass, while the molecular structure of the wine crumbles. "How many farewell tours have Kiss gone on?"

"Isn't endless repetition a kind of end?"

Even in the oblivion of everything that ever was, you smile. "You're catching on."

"I came to get you out."

"That will earn you some trouble."

I shrug, like you. "I was going to clock out, anyway."

All my life, I've believed if you kept your mouth shut, if you blended in, if you followed the rules, then traipsing around in time would have no consequences. That's all bullshit. Every single one of our jumps, our arcs, our twists and turns through this year and that year punched so many holes in them the whole thing just lost its integrity. Time is linear, sure, but time is also unstable. Always has been, just like I had always been in What Cheer, on New Year's 1972. That was true a million years before and it's true now, at the end. This is what the bureau protects. Not the integrity of time, but its inherent variability.

You take my hand. "I'm free now. We both are."

Everything becomes dark. Cold. Numb. "How?"

"Listen."

Creation crumbles around us. Atoms spin off from their nuclei. Molecules undergo massive, sudden change. Elements break down and reform and everything that was, is.

The wine confuses with the glass. My hand. Existence. "I thought this lasted forever."

"It does," you say, light shimmering beneath your skin. "But it's also right now. If you go, you'll be ok. You'll live, and be the same. You'll have a long, good life."

"I don't want to leave you."

"You didn't."

"I want to save you."

"You did."

"Why did you talk to me?"

"So I'd listen."

Stars bloom into pink flowers. Galaxies tick into clock hands. Charcoal pills collapse into black holes. My being confuses with yours. Infinity. Possibility. This is terrifying.

Exhilarating.

I take my shoes off. In an instant, they erupt into supernovas. My socks catch fire. I do.

"Will I ever see you again?"

Your smile stretches across the transmuting universe. The twinkle in your eyes births stars and we are both the fire of the end and the seed of the beginning and there is nothing between life and death, or then and now, but you.

ONE – Dive Bar On Main Street, 1972 (Revisited)

I've been all through time at this point. Time starts to become like all these streaming services. I just scroll forever, searching for something I can't identify. What you're really looking for, it turns out, is yourself. New Year's in What Cheer is a quiet, cold affair. In 1972 it rained, though historical accounts may differ.

This year has been through the wash once or twice.

I'll tell you a secret: they all have. Inside the bar, you don't say anything at first, and neither do I. Rules. Also, what can you say about someone wearing those hideous red pants? Really? But then the magnetic resonance of the end, present in all things, turns the clock hands on my dress.

"What do you think?" I say. "Too much?"

V.M. NELSON

Author.Gamer.Lover Of Fantasy.

Author V.M. Nelson

V.M. NELSON writes young adult and new adult paranormal/fantasy novels. Her debut novel *Hunted* was a Next Generation Indie Book Awards finalist in 2023. She is the author of *The Dhampyr Series* and *Forged of Immortal Blood*. She resides in Minnesota with her partner and three children. When she isn't writing, you can find her playing video games or spending time with the family. If asked, she would prefer to live in an alternative universe with vampires and fairies. Learn more at: **virginiamnelson.com/**

Chapter Four

The Oasis

By: V.M. Nelson

O NE HUNDRED AND NINETY-THREE. That's the number of days I've been living in this small ridiculous room. A room made to lock up an animal. Funny thing, I was the animal. A normal person would lose track of the days, but not me. My brain works differently. The room I call my home is tiny with crisp white walls. Whiter than the plains of Basgah, the province where everything is frozen, and snow never seems to stop falling. I asked my parents if we could go there once when I was eight after hearing someone speak about it during one of my treatments. My father said humans weren't allowed out of the province we lived in. Until then, I didn't know we had our own province. Honestly, at that time, I didn't really know how different we were from the inhabitants of this planet.

A low continuous hum fills the air from the rows of fluorescent lights lining the ceiling. I barely hear it anymore. That unending buzz is a permanent fixture of this cold and sterile place. I wonder if others notice it.

There's a large metal door at one end of my room and a mirror the entire length of the wall at the other. Depending on the day, these beings watch me through it. They don't know it—or at least I think they don't—but I can see them. The only other items in the room are a bed in one corner and a corrosion-resistant alloy toilet and sink. At least that's what it's called here, in this world. My mom once told me that on Earth, they called this material stainless steel. Earth . . . a place I know I'll never see.

The facility I live in is called Oasis. My mother said they named it this because they considered this our refuge—our safe haven. This was their gift to saving humans from a planet they set out to destroy.

My whole life consisted of my parents bringing me to this place once a month so the creatures in the white suits could test me, check my health, and make sure the first human born on Naverea survived. At least that was what I was told. Now I know the truth.

During our excursions, my mother would turn around to look at me as I sat in the back of our vehicle, her eyes swollen and red while my father's remained stony and cold. Once we approached the facility gates, she would say, "Remember, do what you're told, and it will be over quickly." Then she would follow up with, "Trust me, Callie. You can always trust I'm doing what's best for you." I trusted her because she was my mother. I trusted she would take care of me and keep me safe. Now I scoff at the lie, the memory raw in my mind.

I hate this place.

I hate this planet.

I hate these . . . whatever these absurd creatures are.

This planet is considered small compared to others in the galaxy. I was told it was similar to the size of Earth, and the atmosphere is identical. My parents, I hate them too, made a bargain during the discord that began thirty years ago. They would receive safe passage to Naverea—while the Navereans slowly killed off Earth—in exchange for me, their firstborn. As time went on, the Naverean leaders grew dissatisfied in their trade agreement with Earth and decided to remove all their resources at once, making the planet unlivable. That was probably their plan all along. Take the gullible humans they could manipulate and kill off the ones who didn't trust the invaders.

Today, like every other day, this is what I'm thinking about. And just like every other day, I find myself putting one foot in front of the other. Pacing back and forth across the room. Staring at the walls. White—it's all white. Couldn't they have added some color? Blue is nice. Maybe green. But no, it's all just white.

I continue my stroll across the room. They are coming to treat me soon. It happens at the same time every day. They can easily camouflage themselves and blend into the walls, except for the heavily tinted glass that covers their eyes. Like the mirror, I can see through the glass coverings, where I stare at those yellow serpentine eyes. Never do I see any other part of them except for those eyes. Cold-blooded. Wrong.

The door slides open, which is my cue to hop up onto the bed. They never speak, and their movements are jagged, almost robotic. I call them all Bio for no other reason than their suits look like the biohazard suits I saw in a movie once. Today they will take blood like usual and administer my "treatment," the one that allows them some control over me. I know this because it's midweek. When I was young, my parents taught me to count time by Earth standards and to read in English. They said it might come in handy one day to know something other than the Naverean ways. It was also embedded into my head, not to tell anyone I could do it. If others knew they might hurt me. So here I secretly practice counting months, counting days, counting hours. It helps remind me of where I came from.

"What's happening out in Naverea today, Bio?" As usual, silence. "Oh, really? That's good to hear. I was wondering if there was any news about Navereans locking up humans against their will. No? Maybe tomorrow."

I wonder if they will ever talk to me. Nothing I have tried has worked. Even when I press their buttons in hopes of them telling me to shut up, I get nothing. When they first locked me up in this facility, I used to berate them and throw food trays at their heads. I was a pretty good aim but, they didn't like that, and it made things worse. The Bios would call in the hall guards by simply tapping the button on their wrist. I quickly learned how scary the guards in the hall were. Humans altered to do their bidding. Not like me but human, nonetheless. They tied me to my bed and taped my mouth shut. I remember the blank looks in their eyes. Hollow. Empty. Eventually, I gave up on fighting. Humor and sarcasm became my tools for interacting with them and entertaining myself.

"So, what kind of bandage will I get today? Do you have one with an Earth feline on it? Maybe a pink Earth feline? You know, to add a little color and brighten up the place? White is so yesterday."

I roll up my sleeve, preparing for my captor to pull out the usual blood draw kit. Instead, he puts down a tray of food, then turns and walks out the door. I watch as it slides shut, unsure why he has left the room. Until now, they have taken my blood at this time every day. My palms grow damp. I wipe them on my shirt as I stare at the mirror.

Static fills the room, and my eyes land on the glowing red light above the speaker.

"Hello, Callie." The strange voice echoes through the room.

It has been so long since someone said my name, it's like hearing it for the first time. I rub my forehead with my fingers. Memories rush through me.

I am Callie, not just any normal human, like my parents.

I am Callie, the genetically altered girl.

Callie, born for one purpose only.

Callie, born to fulfill the debt incurred by my parents.

Callie the human soldier, who will bend to the will of Naverean leaders to do their bidding.

The truth came out when Oasis became my permanent home. The Navereans were trying to build an army of genetically altered humans. They were willing to waste our lives to preserve their own. We were mere resources to them, tools. I was told that humans were the first aliens to have a genetic makeup similar to the Navereans. The same brain structure, although not as advanced as theirs. When my parents realized this was what my treatments were for—preparing me to kill, to mutilate others, to become one of many clones in the Naverean army—they expressed their regrets and promised to make it better. But better for who? Because living like this—locked in a room without anyone that truly cares for me—isn't better for me. They told me to trust them. What a joke.

My parents tried to kill me 194 days ago. They apologized while telling me I was better off dead. My father tried to choke me against a wall. His face on that day is forever implanted in my memory. A film circling behind my lids on repeat. I see the way the rivers of tears left red streaks down his cheeks. Watch how the snot bubbled from his nose and spit flew into my face as he cried out, squeezing tighter. The worst part is that I can still feel his fingers pressing into my skin. Sometimes I find myself clawing at my throat in the middle of the night, trying to tear those hands off me. Right before what I thought would be my last breath—when the stars crept in under my eyelids—the team of suits broke into our home and stopped him.

I remember the look on my mother's face like it happened this morning. She really thought it was better for me to die than to come here. Maybe she was right because now my parents are dead, and I am Naverean property, nothing more. Sometimes I wonder if I should even call them my parents. They lied to me. They willingly sacrificed me before I was born so they could live on Naverea—a planet unknown to them. Look where that got them. And now here I am, a monster who lives in a white padded room, locked up like an animal. What fun for me.

"Who are you?" I focus on the mirror, molding it like wet sand in my mind to form clear glass and allow me sight into the room behind it. There is no movement, not even a flitting shadow.

"You aren't going to find me behind the mirror, Callie."

They know I can see them. The pounding of my heart presses against my chest, hammering away like metal against a forge. When it reaches my fingertips, I slide my hands under the front of my shirt to hide the way they shake. I don't have the upper hand.

"Do you know why you are here?" asks the voice. Through the static, I can tell it's gruff, older, masculine. "You are meant to become an elite soldier to ensure Naverean rule over all other occupied planets in the solar systems."

"That doesn't sound like a good idea. What if I choose to ignore your orders? Break you into pieces and feed you to the sewer creatures? Then maybe I will rule over your planet and treat your people like you have treated mine."

The speaker crackles, then goes silent.

"Hello?" They can't be done with this conversation. *I'm* not done with this conversation. "Hellllloooo?"

The static returns, and so does the voice. "That is the reason you are here, Callie. We have not been able to find a way to control you. We cannot let you out until you are under our control." Another long pause. "And since your mind is not as disciplined as the others . . ."

The others.

My heart now pounds in my ears. My hearing dulls, and my breathing grows louder. I can hear my pulse inside my head like a ceremonial drum. My lips part, drawing in slow, even breaths, waiting for what is next.

"We have no other choice but to exterminate you. You are a risk to us and to Naverea."

I am right. They aren't going to let me live.

I wipe my hands on my pants, locking up my emotions as best as I can. Acid rises in my throat, burning the flesh as it travels into my mouth and coats my tongue. I push it back into my stomach, rancid, and it leaves a vile taste behind. I cannot show weakness. I will survive.

Like a switch, I turn it off.

"And here I thought I was relaxing in a state-of-the-art spa." The sarcasm flows from my lips as naturally as the sun rises and sets each day. My fear slowly turns to anger. I am angry at myself for becoming complacent and angry at the people I once called Mom and Dad. "Answer me one question, great and powerful creature hiding behind the veil. What does *exterminate* actually mean to you? Will I be dropped off on an island to live in solitude or burn in a fiery pit somewhere?"

In return, all I hear is silence.

I am to be destroyed. There is no way they will let me go, set me up with a new home and a new job while we both know I might be able to level a community if I am at full strength. Energy pulses through my veins. It furiously pushes against my skin like the waves along the Mawen seashore. I remember the way the ocean water crashed against the rocks, exploding into frothy suds which sprayed into the air. That is how my insides feel right now. Explosive. Ready to rage and wipe out everything in my path.

Breathing in deeply, I find myself staring at the petite girl in the mirror, trying to bring her back. She is me. I move closer to get a better look. Realization blankets me. At some point, I stopped caring. I started accepting that this was my fate, my future. I touch the mirror as if to reach for myself. Instead, I ball my hand into a fist, draw my arm back, and punch my reflection. *You stupid girl. You gave up. You let them win.* The glass rattles hard, but it doesn't break. My breath is fast. I know I need to calm down before I give them a reason to come in and strap me to the bed like they used to. One time they couldn't pin me down because electricity bled out of my fingertips. That was when I started receiving my treatments. I believe whatever is in those treatments subdues my power, makes me docile.

I step back. The last thing I want to do is show them that my power is still bristling inside me. A single tear runs down my cheek as I lie down on the bed and stare at the blank ceiling.

Don't give them a reason to come in here. Pretend you are weak.

The Navereans love to belittle humans. They love to see us in pain, and more importantly, they love to see us fall at their feet. This is my wake-up call. It's time to get out of here. Time to plan my escape.

The lights go out at the same time every night. I wait patiently, going through the plan in my mind. The codes used to get in and out of the rooms are reset every thirty days. I've always kept track of the numbers in case it came in handy. Today it is coming in handy. I can remember everything I hear, recall the tones of the buttons. I know the code to my door will remain 109731 for one more week. Not that it matters, because I am leaving tonight.

Two clicks, and the lights go off. Now the guards will start making their rounds. There is always a delay between the second guard and the third. That's when I will act. After the second makes his rounds, I will open the door. Every room is marked with a letter of the English alphabet. I think them using the alphabet was intentional, a way to make the parents who brought their children here feel more at home. Another façade.

My breathing quickens, knowing that once I pass room A, there will be a set of double doors. Through those doors, my freedom.

There was a time when I believed my abilities made me abnormal in a bad way. I didn't want to be different. Now I am glad I have these abilities, because they will allow me to change my fate. Even if those traits have been muted by the treatments, I know I can use them to my advantage.

I hear the guard now. He stands outside the door. He will stay there for a few more moments, slide open the metal eye slot, peek in, then move on. The scrape of metal as the small window closes is my signal. Quietly, I stand up. It's time to go.

I enter the code on the keypad. The door slides open, and I slip into the hall like a creature prowling in the night, looking for its next meal. It takes less than a second for my eyes to adjust from the dark room to the lighted hallway. The guard is checking a door down the hall, so I duck back inside my room. With my eyes tightly closed I count to three before trying again and see him round the corner. Carefully, I move back into the hall. The flickering lights above my head keep me alert as I type the code into the keypad. The door slithers shut and I'm one step closer to freedom.

I stay on the balls of my feet and glance at the letter on my door—K. Hugging the wall, I glide along in my white socks. I see the next door—J. I pass by it while listening for any sounds that might alert the guards.

Exterminated.

I cannot get caught. If I do, I will take as many Navereans as possible down with me.

Exterminated.

Part of turning me into a killing machine was giving me heightened strength and agility. The Navereans may have muted my special abilities with their treatments, but the basic ones remain, dull but still flitting through me, waiting for me to release them.

Exterminated.

No, they will not dictate whether I live or die. I will choose and I choose to live.

I see another door and a camera on the ceiling down the hall. It is pointed around the corner, then slowly begins to swivel. I inch closer to the door marked I, leaning into it as best I can. Why didn't I think about cameras? Doesn't matter. I can't let it faze me. I just need to figure it out, because I can't go back.

I push my body hard against the door and look around. There are no windows. The next door down isn't a sliding door with a letter. Instead, it has a handle and a picture of . . . I squint. "Mopper," I breathe—the robotic mopping machine that comes through to do the floors once a month. It's a supply closet.

I check the camera. If I can get into that room in the next few seconds, I can hide. I'll wait until the camera is pointed at the farthest corner, and then I just need to run. Maybe I'll make it to the front door before it swivels back toward me. Even if I don't, I should be able to get out before someone catches me. I take a deep breath and get ready to run for the closet.

Click.

The door labeled I slides open. I fall backward into the room and land on my backside. There is a face hovering over me.

"What's up, buttercup?" The gritty voice grinds along my skin. I jump up and pull at his shirt to move him out of the way, but he pushes me back. He seals the door behind me and leans against it, arms crossed over his chest.

"Let me out. I am running out of time." Who is this guy? The third guard will be here soon. I need to go.

"First tell me what you are up to," says the mysterious young man. "It looks like you are trying to escape, and if so, I'm coming along."

"Wait, are you speaking English?"

He chuckles and bows sardonically. "You aren't the only human in here, princess. I'll say it again—I'm coming with you."

He can't come with me. I have to go *now*. The burn under my skin flares with urgency. "I really don't have time for this," I say. I shove him, but it's like trying to move a mountain. My arms drop to my sides in defeat.

He presses his hand into my chest. "It's really not a hard concept. You and I leave my room and escape. Together."

He's serious. I gather my thoughts and remember they have one goal. They are going to exterminate me. "Fine, whatever. Just open the door. The third guard will be making his rounds soon. He is going to catch us if we wait."

The young man quickly turns toward the door, punching the code into the keypad. The door skates open. When I try to look out into the hall, he pulls me back, pinning me against the wall. He leans against me. The light outside the room softly illuminates his features. My breath catches. He is my age, and when he smiles at me, my heart flutters like the wings of a dragonfly. We realize it at the same time.

"You are like me," he says. "An altered human. Did your parents put you in here as well? Something about a better life in Naverea and only needing to give up one kid?"

I look at him closer. He's *exactly* like me.

"Yeah, that's me—Callie the experimental super soldier who cannot be controlled and now must perish." One might think I would keep the dramatics to a minimum in my final hours, but nah. I'm still irritated by my parent's actions and how self-centered they were to save themselves and sacrifice me.

"Call me Caleb, the rehab failure about to be terminated." He places his finger under my chin and lifts my face so our eyes meet. "And I thought I was the only one left."

I see the same betrayal deep in his eyes that I see in mine whenever I look in that stupid mirror. Selfish parents, mutated body, death at our door. "Well, Caleb, it's nice to meet you, but we need to get out of here. We can't stick around here counting the days to our execution."

A flash of acknowledgment crosses his features. "We each thought we were alone, but there are two of us. Should we look for others?" He leans out into the hall, then pulls back to meet my eyes again.

The realization of what he's saying causes a furrow in my brow. My voice drops to a whisper. "We can't. We don't have time." Now I'm being the selfish one, but I know—and I know he knows—that this is our only chance.

"Right. I just thought . . ." He pauses, then gives one sharp nod, and I see the ferocity return to his face. He grabs my hand, still looking at me. "We should bypass the storage room. The camera will catch us either way. We need to just run. I need you to trust me, okay? Don't stop. Don't look back. Just run as fast as your unnatural ability allows."

He sticks his head out into the hall again.

Trust him? Trust him to change my plan to his. The closet will keep me safe from the cameras. The closet is where I can hide. Everyone I know has betrayed me. What if he's about to do the same? What if he's setting me up for his gain?

He tugs my arm, but I keep my feet planted and refuse to move.

"What's the problem? I thought we decided we have to go."

"How can I trust you?" I snatch my hand away from him. "Trust is earned. You have done nothing to earn my trust." It's as if bugs crawl on my skin. Moving along my arms, my back, and legs, creating a vortex of unease. My parents always told me I should trust them. I did and look where I ended up.

The lines around his eyes soften. "Callie. Everyone has betrayed not only you but me too. I have no one to trust either, so I am choosing to trust you to help me get out of this nightmare. Will you do the same and trust me just for a little while? When we get out, if you want to go your own way, you can." He brushes a few loose strands of my hair behind my ear.

My shoulders relax for the first time. Do I really have a choice? I need to go, and if it turns out he's lying, I will just have to kill him too. "Okay. I'll trust you. But if you betray—"

"I know, I know. You will put me through a grater and shred me into pieces."

I knit my brow, blinking at him. "How—"

"Strength, agility, and telepathy. Now, let's go."

I slip my hand back into his. "Of course you trust me—you can read my thoughts like a flashing billboard," I mumble under my breath.

He smirks and peeks out the door again. Then he takes off, and I follow him, running as fast as I can.

We round the corner and pass rooms H, G, F, and E. My heart races—four rooms left, and then we are free. But where will we go once we get outside? The thought is like a load of heavy bricks on my shoulders. I think and run. I run and think. And then I remember the sewers. My parents used to show them to me when I was little. The facility sat along a lake. After my treatments my parents would take me down to the water to skip stones. I used to think it was weird that they would point out the sewers every time we were there. Now it makes me wonder . . . were they setting me up for this moment? If we were going to have any chance of survival, Caleb and I need to make it to that grate.

We reach the end of the hall and dart around the next corner, avoiding the camera, then slide to an abrupt halt. Two burly men wearing all black and holding batons that glow white at one end are standing in the hall. The batons crackle and spark. The guards are right in front of the double doors, bouncing their pulsing batons against their hands in unison, just like clones. The fire burns within me, blazing against my bones. My thirst for freedom grows. I shift my gaze to the moonlight shining through the small windows behind them.

The guards stop moving and focus on us, eyes growing larger than saucers as they take us in.

"Stop right there!" one of the men yells as the other one reaches over and slams his hand against the emergency button. Sirens blare and red lights churn violently as they run toward us.

Caleb glances at me. "You take out righty. I got lefty. No matter what happens, we are free tonight, Callie." He pauses and lowers his voice. "And if anything happens to me, keep going. No hero moves."

I quickly nod, keeping my focus on the men. "Same for you." It is time to use whatever superstrength I have to get out of here.

Running as fast as I can, I go straight for my guy. My foot connects with his forearm, knocking the baton from his grasp. It spirals across the floor behind him, the sparks brightening each time it hits a wall. The guard grunts and grabs me by my shoulders, then headbutts me. I land on my back and clutch my head, which spins like a toy whirling on its pointed edge. I try my best to shake it off. The man grabs me by my ponytail, pulling me along the floor.

I close my eyes and let the charge inside me dart through my veins like a runaway train. It scrapes against every inch of my flesh. Bolts of lightning hover at my fingertips. I don't hesitate—reaching back to grab the man's arm, I pull him over my shoulder. He crashes down, taking a handful of my hair with him. I scramble to my feet, noticing he looks shocked by my strength. I feel power bleeding out of my pores. My hair stands on end, a slight reverberation dancing along my skin.

Out of the corner of my eye, I can see Caleb, fast and fierce. If he's reading his opponent's mind, he knows what the guard is going to do before he does it.

I hear faint footsteps echoing in the hall behind us. More guards are coming. My guy is back on his feet. I charge him this time and knock him onto his back, then punch him directly in the nose. The crackling electricity within me jolts through my arm and into him. He grabs his face, rolling around and crying out.

Backing away, I turn to help Caleb, but he grabs my hand and pulls me toward the door. The approaching guards are fast, the thumping of their feet barely audible over the blaring sirens.

"Hurry, Callie!"

We run past the final four doors—D, C, B, and finally A. The alarm keeps blaring in my ears. The swirling red lights seem to rotate more urgently. I look over my shoulder and see the guards behind us getting closer. One more door to go—the front door—and it cannot come fast enough.

"Caleb, we need to use our strength to break down this door, otherwise we won't make it!"

We turn toward each other, take a deep breath, and jump shoulder-first into the door. The cold slab of steel flies off its hinges, and we skid along the dirt pathway on top of it. Within seconds, the cool breeze wraps itself around my body, hugging me.

I want to lie here and rest, especially as I feel my body begin to return to normal. The currents that raced through me moments ago, slicing through my flesh, subside. All I want to do now is stare up at the stars like I used to do, but there is no time. They are still coming for us.

Caleb is on his feet already. "Come on, Callie. Get up."

I take the hand of the boy who is just like me and pull myself up. He is the boy I trusted. The one who didn't let me down. Perhaps the only person in the world I can relate to.

We run.

I know the hard part is just beginning. We are on a planet we know very little about, though we have called it home since we were born. A planet that turned us into mistakes and now wants to exterminate us.

We will run from the Navereans, who treat humans as objects, who dispose of others as easily as if they're taking out the trash. We will run until we are ready to fight And one day, rest assure we will be ready to fight.

"That way. There are sewers on the north end of the lake."

"I'm aware." He gives me a slight smirk.

"We are going to need to talk about you being in my head when we stop running."

"Yes, princess."

I take one last look back as Caleb pulls the metal grate off the sewer. The guards are far enough away for me to know we are free from this facility, but we will be running for that freedom for quite some time.

"Ready?" Caleb reaches for my hand. I can see the relief on his face. "Do you trust me?"

"I do." I smile my first genuine smile in months.

TR NICKEL
Literary Fantasy Author

Author TR Nickel

TR NICKEL (TRN) released her debut novel, *Light of Evanora* (of the *Legends of Limoria Series*), in 2021. Known by friends and family for her intense imagination and a desire to make others smile, TRN has been fascinated with creating something magical since childhood. What began with poetry that she would jot down into a tiny bright yellow memo pad grew into a passion to fill a world with her own craziness. TRN also serves as one half of Red Rose Words alongside fellow author Jeri "Red" Shepherd (read more in Jeri's bio after her story). Learn about TR Nickel's worlds at: **www.trnickel.com/**

CHAPTER FIVE
The Shadow Harmony
By: TR Nickel

THE ASSIGNMENT

S ERAPHINA 'BLACKTHORN' WELLINGTON

I move through the city's labyrinthine alleys like a wraith, my silhouette blending with the shadows that cling to the buildings. The night air crackles with an electric energy as bars and clubs blast music, and the distant hum of traffic creates a rhythmic backdrop to my silent steps. Tall skyscrapers loom overhead, their windows aglow with the iridescence of neon signs. The Pit is a sprawling expanse where magic and the mundane intertwine, a dance of secrets and mysteries hidden isn plain sight. Built up from a crater when the world leaders-of a life long past-decided that killing each other was better than talking things out. Those who couldn't reach the Underground were mutated by the radiation from the bombs into creatures that could only be described as mythical monstrosities. Through generations, the people living under the crust began being born with unspeakable powers; the radiation being administered even far below the surface.

Magic was no longer a fantasy.

Nearly a decade has passed since the resurface occurred, the Pit becoming what it is. The only thing keeping the monsters at bay for us here is a radioactive ring. Shadows Harmony. The name makes me wanna gag. It's so cheesy. The thing keeps the balance; we get it. No one quite understands how or why it even works, but it keeps a barrier up-the kind where, when those things try to get through, they just turn away.

No mess to clean up or waste of bullets.

The city is still crawling with monsters, though, just ones who are more human than beast.

Some consider me one of those monsters. I never much minded the constant battle of leaning into the magic that radiated from the earth and the fight to maintain tradition-whatever that is. My philosophy is to do what you have to, but at least do it with flair. Nothing is worse than someone having a crap personality on top of loose morals. I'm not one of the Extra Gifted Beings, but I use the magic items they or the planet produce. I mean, who wouldn't go for magical bullets that can change based on what you want them to do?

Navigating the urban maze, communities built in skyscrapers that nearly lean onto one another. My eyes flicker to the ticket booth. Bullet proof glass, bars, and only a tiny slot for money and verification of purchase to slip through.

His yellowed eyes lock with mine. "You're late." Gerrick grumbles, his voice muffled from his little cage.

"Was nothing personal, promise." I smile at him, placing my hands on the counter. "You have my ticket?"

His sickly green scaled hand slides a ticket through the hole. "You know she hates it when you're late." I take the small piece of parchment, pursing my lips for a moment before my resting smirk returns. There is a faint click from under Gerrick's desk as I walk to the theatre doors.

This is the only way to really survive here. Bored-job. Hungry-job. Want people to leave you alone? Job. Fear is a great motivator and deterrent, and when you are a phantom like I am-well, people don't really want to risk being haunted.

I open the doors, bright but flickering lights illuminate the lobby. If I hadn't become accustomed to harsh lights like this, the brightness might be bothersome, but The Pit relies on what radiation remains for its electricity. That's the public stance, anyway. I've seen the actual way this city powers itself, and whoever designed that thing is the biggest monster of all of us.

"Weren't you just here?" A familiar voice calls out, Blindspot standing up from behind the snack counter. "You couldn't have gone through your rations that quickly."

"That was a few days ago, Pots." They knit their brows together as I walk up to them.

Their pale eyes are unable to focus on me. I carefully reach over the counter, grabbing a few of the ration cards.

"Stop calling me that." Blindspot scolds me, gripping my wrist and making me drop the cards.

I laugh it off, ripping myself out of their grasp. "I'll make a mental note."

"That'll be the fifth one." They slap down one of the ration cards in front of me.

My eyes roll, hearing such a stern tone come from them. They need to learn how to lighten up. The boss is only scary when she wants something. I hope they realise that before they waste their lives taking themselves too seriously.

Picking up the card, I head to theatre one. "You and Gerrick should go out sometime. I think it'll help get those sticks out of your-." A knife whisks past my ear, impaling the wall in front of me. I turn back, "Fine, I'll drop it."

"Make sure that mental note sticks." They hiss, a golden hue illuminating their pale stare.

My smirk widens and I rip the knife out of the wall, pocketing it as a little souvenir from my favourite ration keeper. The hue fades and they go back to whatever it was they were doing.

Strutting down the hall, I startle one of the 'ticket keepers' as he didn't hear me approaching behind him. I give him a wink. He immediately glares, but it softens as the tiny gears in his brain turn and the recognition kicks in.

"Blackthorn," He mutters, reaching backwards and opening the door for me.

I glance down at the name stitched into his candy striped uniform. "Mike." He nods, taking my ticket.

The interior is dark, only illuminated somewhat by the bright screen that has snakes slithering around on it. The same stop motion movie that is always playing in this room. I walk to the heart of the chamber, all the seats empty. I look back at the screen, but with a whistle, I turn back to see the paneling on the back wall opens up.

"Perhaps you should ask if she'll throw in a watch with this next payment." Kilby and his smug smirk, makes mine drop.

I walk up the stairs, his eyes following my movements like I'm the movie that's screening. "Maybe you should ask her to get you deodorant." I tease, shoving past him and through the small opening.

The room is lit by green and blue neon signs, armed guards scattered around, some sitting at the round tables covered in firearms. Others at the bar top with large screens showing that they are shifting money around to different people Viper employs. Some known criminals, while others are politicians, a few on the force, most of them I don't recognise.

"If it isn't my favourite little rat." A behemoth of a man with not a single hair adorning his head steps out of the way, letting me see her.

She has the crime boss look down. A tattoo of the same snake she's named after surrounds her right eye, her ornamental glass one acting as the Viper's throat.

"How sweet." I give her a forced smile and walk up to her. Everyone's eyes now turned towards us.

She stands, snapping her fingers. Brainiac, the five-foot shorty, walks over, her hands always looking cold and body shaking.

"Did you not get the gloves I sent you?" My voice makes her jump, but she smiles, pushing her glasses up further on her nose.

"I did, thank you." She mutters under her breath.

"Wear them." I state, taking the data pad she's been holding. She just nods and bows out. I look at the boss and shake my head. "She's gonna die of hypothermia."

Viper laughs, "I offered to get her a heater," she raises her hands. "Doesn't want to be an inconvenience."

I unlock the pad as it scans my thumbprint. Pictures of a gaudy ring popping up, the Server building where most of the city's dangerous or unknown experiments are located, and some of the guard postings. My jaw clenches as I glare up at Veronica.

I scoff. "What was it you called me? Your favourite? Sending me on a suicide mission doesn't scream love to me." I toss the assignment onto her desk.

"We have a high paying client. It's not without its rewards." Viper says, shrugging her shoulders, her smile widening. I raise a brow, waiting for the magic words. "Your payout would be nearly half a million quid, kid."

My eyes widen, laughing in disbelief. I place my hands behind my head, just thinking about what I could do with that money. This could get out of this hellhole. I wouldn't have to fight for every crumb I get.

"Mother earth, that is...Okay, yeah." I mutter, grabbing the data pad once again. "You really know how to persuade a person." Veronica chuckles.

"It's a true blessing." She says, taking her seat. "You're the best of the best. If someone could get in and out without dying, it would be you."

"Glad to have your confidence." I bite my lip, trying to contain the excitement of receiving that payload. "I'm going to need at least ten per cent up front."

"As always." Her eyes watch me intently, and I assume most would feel the pressure of her gaze, but I grew up with those eyes trained on me.

The Viper and I go way back, all the way to my adolescents. Talk about having a superb role model. I know what she expects out of me. I've seen the bottom of her boot enough times to have it built in like muscle memory. One day, when she's had enough or someone plans a coup d'état, she'll name me the successor. Not that she has told me this, but like I said, I know what's expected out of me.

My eyes run over the data, taking in the different access points, our contact, different encryptions they use, everything that makes this-somewhat-possible.

"First impressions?" My eyes flicker upward to meet her gaze.

"I think I'll buy a car first. Practical and fun." I mumble, looking back down and continuing to read.

She leans forward; the desk creaking under the shifting of weight. "Sera." I look up at her once more. Her gaze, resembling a pool of venom.

"I can do it." The definiteness makes her eyes widen. "I've never failed before. I don't see why I'd start now."

"Good." Veronica, her widening smile hidden slightly under her clasped hands.

THE HEIST

Seraphina 'Blackthorn' Wellington

The Pits restlessness pulses, echoing through the streets as I navigate through the lively crowd. Bodies bumping against one another, making it easy for my hands to roam. I steal ration cards, watches, rings, anything I can snatch. In a crowd like this, I avoid any recognition. The club I live above works well, alive during my working hours and access to the necessities like people's pockets. It's been a week and I am brushing up against my deadline. Viper was worried I'd rush this, and perhaps that fear is from my beginner days. I had no hesitation when I was younger, but I was desperate back then.

I'm not that little girl anymore.

Pushing past the people entering, I see myself reflected in the glass. My black hair braided back, exposing my pale skin. After this, I could take a break, maybe see the sun now and again. Might be nice not living in the shadows. I kick out the wheels hiding in the heels of my shoes, stealing a ride by grabbing the tail of the car driving by. I glide over the pavement, my destination far from the entertainment district. It's not the worst place to be here in the Pit, but it's not great. I like to think most people who live here have the same philosophy I do. Otherwise, I'm not sure why anyone would willingly hang around street corners or deal with the bluefins when they deign to come visit us from their teched out skyscrapers. The centre of the city is nothing but posh people who deem themselves better. It's mostly descendants of the first crest dwellers who came topside. Living on top of the entrance to the Underground.

"You wanna ride? Pay for it!" The cabbie shouts out the window, as we stop at a red bulb.

I let go, offering a smile. "Just needed to get closer to the tram."

"Damn grifters." He mumbles, rolling up his window.

Weaving through the cars on the road, I make my way to the pavement. The line for the tram is already building up as I jog over. My eyes glance towards the people not waiting, but lined up against the wall. Skinnier than I am, and bodies slumped in ways that I'm sure are the only way they can get comfortable. I grab the rations in my pocket and hand them out. Their eyes all widen and they say blessings I don't need, but I take them anyway. By the time the line has made its way into the tight corridors of the roughly welded together transport, I just hop on, grabbing the loading rail.

The plan I've thrown together is not what's driving my confidence right now. It has to be quick, and I won't be able to repeat anything twice. I'm bringing everything I've got for this one, and I doubt it's anywhere near enough. Viper offered some men for a portion of my cut, but I dismissed it. A job like this would fail with brute force, and besides that, I always work best alone.

A part of me is quite eager to see just how far my skill can carry me, and how much luck I have left to make it out with more than just my life. Therein lies my confidence. I'm like a cat with nine lives, and I've maybe only used half of them. The biggest advantage I have is the little tip I gave my old pal Investigator Hale. Despite being one of the few clean cops, I know he's been trying to sniff me out for the past few months. I'm not sure what one of my hits got him hooked, but I'm quite the obsession, it seems. Would be a good way to get promoted, which is why I know that the rest of the fuzz is going to be far from the scene of the crime. He's making my job so easy. So greedy he won't want to share the score of bringing me in.

Hopping off the tram, I head to the rendezvous place of our contact. Pulling up my mask, bending the soft metal to mould to the bridge of my nose, holding the dark fabric in place. I scan my surroundings before reaching towards the fire ladder that'll lead me up the side of 2246 N Lament Rd. As I crest the top, a man is standing near the edge. The rusted bar acting as safety railing comes up to his torso.

"You're e-early." He stutters, turning to look at me. His hand is gripping the railing. "I want you-u to know. I'm, I'm only doing this because they d-deserve it."

"Yeah?" I keep my tone plain as I continue my approach.

He nods, swallowing hard. "Th-the things they are doing there...It's horrible." I tilt my head a bit.

This was not in the data given. Disgruntled was the word they used, but this seems more vindictive.

"Horrible things that would affect me in there?" I ask, now face to face with him.

He has sweat dripping down his brow, "Maybe not directly,"

"Then we will have to skip the backstory for now." I cut him off, extending my hand. "Type it up. I'll digest it later."

The contact lets out a shaky breath, pulling out an ID bracelet and dropping it in my hands. "You'll have ten minutes before the building's AI registers that your biometrics do not match with the ID's owner."

I eye him up and down as I clasp the bracelet on. He's wearing a white lab coat, a button up and slacks. His body tenses, from seeing my gaze.

"I'll need your coat." I mutter, pulling my black leather jacket off my shoulders and tossing it on one of the air vents. "Gotta blend in."

He nods and strips out of it, handing it to me. I adorn it. It's oversized, perfect for hiding the arsenal I wear across my body.

"What are you planning to do?" He takes a step back, my eyes shifting to meet his.

"Does it matter?" He shakes his head and looks away. "Didn't think so."

The Server building shines like a beacon, my ticket to an easier life. A blue hue it emanates casts a haze all around it. Guards surround the place, all with their weapons out in the open to let me know what they are packing. Yay for me.

I strut towards the entrance, knowing that there's no bailing out once I walk through that door. I activate my expensive -but well worth the investment- altervail. Shifting my face to that of a doe-eyed lady and not the siren I am. Can't risk someone here remembering what I look like or noting my features later on. I hold out my wrist to the ID scanner to the right of the door, a blue light scanning the bracelet. One guard glances my way, just as the doors slide open.

The guard smiles towards me, giving me a once over. I give him an innocent look, making him smile wider. This is exactly why this face is my go to for inside jobs. No one questions a person who draws attention, especially one who has such angelic features. Growing up with a snake gave me sharp eyes that people become defensive around. Like they know I can see right through them.

"Welcome, Mrs Landry." A woman at the front desk stands and greets me.

I give her a wave and a smile. She sits back down. Perhaps it was my steps posing such a purpose or the nonchalant effort of my actions that just caused her to break protocol. She skipped the verification, checking the facial ID to match with what's on file. I don't know if I should award that win to my skill or luck.

Walking up to the lift, I push the up button. I glance up, watching as the numbers start to decrease, a gentleman coming up behind me. The doors open and we both step in, hitting our desired floors.

"Gotta love these late nights, right?" He says. I briefly raise my eyes, his purple irises drawing most of my attention. The rest of his features are quite plain.

"Third day this week." I chuckle, looking forward once more.

He hums, "It's my fourth."

I wince and intake a sharp breath, playing into the dread he seems to want to complain about. Must be terrible having something so stable.

"Yikes." I say, shaking my head.

"Lucky for us, though, tomorrow is the end of the week." He mutters, his voice getting deeper. "Maybe we could use the early release to get a drink sometime?"

I shift my gaze back up to meet his, cocking my brow. His purple irises are now a deep red. Mood changing eyes is such a stupid power. Poor fella.

"Wish I could, but I'm afraid Frank from accounting already beat you to it." The door opens to his floor, his gaze shifting to a blue. "Maybe next week." I wink at him as he steps off, walking backwards.

"Oh, what was your name?" He asks, his mood perking up.

Pausing for a moment, opening my mouth just as the doors start to close. "My name is-" The doors cut me off, and I roll my eyes. I change my mind. Once this is over, I need to alter this face just a tad. This is too much attention. Are they all deprived or something?

The floors tick by as I make my way to the centre of the building. The thirty-fifth floor. I glance down at my watch. I only have three minutes before the place goes on lock down. The elevators will be useless and my bracelet won't allow me access anywhere. Worst part of it all is there is nowhere to hide. Server's AI can see any living thing in here, likely the magical essence of the artefacts they keep here as well. Every movement, action, task will have to be perfect.

The elevator stops, a tall woman stepping inside, glancing at me before turning her attention to her data pad, a shorter man pushing a medical cart in behind her.

"XGB-134 is next." She whispers towards him.

He sighs, reaching down to the lower carriage of his cart, grabbing a few needles. "We will need these, then." He mutters back.

They look like sedatives. I focus forward, being aware of every movement they make while trying to maintain my composure. What kind of artefact needs something to knock it out?

She chuckles and nods. "Quite the temperament, that one."

The doors slide open, and they leave, and I let out a sigh. Maybe I should have taken the contact's intel about what exactly is happening here. They are dealing with more than just magical items, that's for sure. I shake my head. It doesn't matter what they are doing. Not right now. All I am here to do is get the Shadows Harmony and get out. It's already a pretty enormous task. Only trying to steal the one item that is creating a semblance of peace for the Pit. Who wanted this thing again? Damn, I really need to reevaluate my morals once I'm out of here.

The elevator slows, but the doors don't open. I glance down at my watch and see one minute remaining, but I think my cover is blown. Whipping out my gun, I shoot the camera in the centre of the lift. Lucky for me, I only need to go up a single floor.

"Gotta move." I use the railing to reach the service hatch on the ceiling.

Shoving it to the side, I pull myself up and on top. Taking a glance around, the easy way out is through the vents, and I can use the ladder to get to my floor. Thank mother earth for having someone on the inside.

I take out my multi-tool, making quick work of unscrewing the vent cover. I let it drop, not bothering to keep quiet at this point. Sliding into the opening, I crawl through, passing by the overhead duct that drops me into the hallway. Nothing like a superhero landing to boost one's confidence. I look at the nearest plaque.

"Light Dancer." I stick my tongue out and grimace.

Hate the name, but I'm sure it does something cool.

I walk down the hall, reading the plaques as I go, when a heavyset woman steps out in front of me. I give her a smile, but she raises her gun.

"Don't. Move." I glance down, seeing the large stance. "You are trespassing on government property!"

I nod, taking a step forward with my hands up. "Yeah, yeah I am."

She furrows her brows and I charge at her, sliding between the guard's legs, ripping off the ID bracelet she's wearing. I get up, turning around just long enough to throw a small disk, it landing on the rear of her neck before continuing forward. A jolt of electricity runs through her body, bringing her down to her knees. I head to the next hallway, running my eyes over the plaques, as I hear a door burst open and the footsteps following it.

"There you are." I mutter, seeing Shadows Harmony etched in the metal plate.

Swiping the guard's bracelet over the scanner on the vault door, unlocks the keypad. I take out my decoder and connect it to the pad.

The machine hums as it runs through its programming, and I dive into the small alcove to take shelter from those who are running into the hallway. I pull out my gun, aiming it for the entrance, being mindful of the elevator behind me on the other side of the hall. Shots are being fired off, the plaster from the wall scattering across the floor and white dust filling the air. I throw one of my daze grenades towards them.

"Take cover!" A guard shouts. I take their advice and cover my eyes. A whirring sound echoes through the hall and I can see the white of the light of the grenade, even through my hands, but it doesn't faze me much.

The machine chimes, and the door opens slightly, letting me know it's time to move. I lean forward, firing off a few shots, causing the guards to retreat into the other hall. Keeping my gun raised, I walk backwards into the vault; grabbing my gear on the way in. The ring, bathed in a reddish glow, rests on a pedestal and inside a bulletproof case. My breath caught as she beheld its beauty – an intricate fusion of metal and magic.

I retrieve the key Viper provided me before I left the theatre, the final piece to the puzzle in making this assignment even possible. The case unlocks and I grab the artefact, feeling a faint hum resonate through my fingertips. I slide the ring on, knowing from experience how backstabbing a pocket can be. I rush to the eastern side, dodging a bullet or two that grazes my arms as I try to avoid being directly shot. Turning the corner, I see my one way out. They will be monitoring the vents since the AI would have told them I crawled through, the elevator is down and they are barricading the staircases. As much as I don't like heights, I have to see this as an area for improvement.

I pull out my grappling hook and glance towards the window I plan on diving out of. This is such a stupid idea, but it's what'll get me out. My hands finish securing the hook to the railing. All that's left to do is jump out this window and fight off Mr Investigator, who will probably be waiting for me.

Easy-peasy, I'm sure.

I shake my head, charging forward towards my exit. I raise my gun, take two shots, close my eyes, before my shoulder slams into the webbed glass. The window gives way. That feeling of falling makes my stomach flip and eyes shoot open. I grab the rope and brace my feet to push off the approaching building. Sweat and a bit of blood drips down my brow as I make my descent. The glass cut my face, which means it deactivated my mask. My reflection confirms that as I pass by windows. Brainiac is going to have to fix it, again.

THE CHASE

Investigator Adrian Hale

I have been hunting her for months, and I am going to catch her. When I received a tip about the hit on Shadows Harmony, there was no doubt in my mind that Viper would send the Blackthorn. My entire career is riding on this, though. If the commissioner finds out I've been sitting on this kind of intel and I come out empty-handed, it'll cost me everything, neck included.

My phone buzzes in my pocket. I pull it out and answer it. "You got Hale."

"Sir, she's here, or at least someone is here." Stanley's words rush out of him. "She's fast. Even with the AI, she knows what she is doing, sir."

"Stanley, take a breath. Do as I told you. Restrict her access. Flood the stairs, she can't use the elevators, and-"

"She is using the vents!" I roll my eyes.

His panicking is going to give me a headache at this point. How did he get the gig for the head of security? This is why politics makes no sense to me. Action is the only thing that matters. No one should give a damn about words.

"Focus, Stanley." I scold. "If she does something, don't let her do it twice." I hang up the phone and hop out of my car.

Slamming the door shut, I look up at the Server building with a smile. Soon she's going to be cornered. No way out, except one. Straight out the thirty-fifth window on the eastside. It's the only side that doesn't have a stairwell. Being as notorious as she is, I doubt she would have come to such a tall tower without being prepared to jump out of it.

I jog over to where all my prepping has led me to, glancing up at the tower's side. As much as I hate to admit it, she's got guts. She either is extremely confident, or is reckless. Either way, I'll be ready for her. I tuck myself into the corner of the building, the decorative frame creating the perfect cubby hole.

"You got this, Hale." I breathe out, readying my gun.

This had to have been an inside job. For her to get into the building without notice. The hallways are tight, which means it doesn't matter how many men you have. She can bottleneck them as she does what she has to. The Viper was really ready for this one, and sending her was the best choice. She works well in high-risk situations. After studying Blackthorn's hits, I could almost admire her for how good she is at her job, but her job is being a criminal and that makes it a pointless thing to be good at.

The sound of glass shattering draws my eyes upward. My eyes widen, seeing her dive out of the window. Her form is rehearsed. The way she turns and utilises her body is not from simple talent. She is better trained than most of our swat team from how she's scaling down the place.

Blackthorn's feet land hard against the concrete. Glass shards falling beside her. Her hands are nimble and untie her from her harness in under a second.

"For a master thief, you sure are predictable." My words cause her to freeze as she turns to focus on me. I emerge from the shadows, my gun locked and loaded; and pointed right at her.

She raises her fists, her breathing laboured from the nonstop movement. "You know, it's rude to point your gun at someone. It's a horrible first impression." I see her grip tighten a bit.

A glow shimmers through the cracks of her fingers in my peripheral.

"The only impression I need is your fingerprint, Blackthorn. I'm taking you in." Despite her staring down the end of a barrel, she doesn't seem phased.

She nods. "I was just telling someone that I was needing a holiday." A smirk resting on her lips.

"Well, isn't that lucky for both of us." I advance towards her, careful steps to be prepared for anything she may try. "I have a cosy little cell with your name on it. Won't have any need for work there."

Reaching down, I grab the cuffs off my belt and bring them up. Being this close gives me a chance to see her features. Not some blurred photograph of her. Those green eyes are sharper than her cheekbones, and her skin is porcelain. A small little scar on her right brow. The glass cut her up, and must've had a few close calls while up there based on the grazes on her lab coat.

"I was thinking something a little less chromatic." She chuckles.

I smile. "Maybe I could get you a poster, liven the place up a bit." I reach up to grab her wrist, but she twists mine instead.

My finger pulls the trigger, but she's moved behind me, shoving my arm up my back. I twist my body, sweeping my foot to kick her legs out from under her. I bring my gun up to point at her, but her foot kicks it from my grasp. She swirls around on the ground, bringing her feet under her. She tilts her head, and I reach for the knife on my belt.

"What's that saying?" She asks, reaching behind her and pulling out a modified Springfield pistol. "Don't bring a knife to a gunfight?" I can feel the sweat on my brow drip.

She's better than I thought. Blackthorn raises her gun, but I charge, connecting with her torso. The sting of the bullet grazes my ear, but it's the ringing that makes me wince. We hit the ground and I grab her wrist. Another round goes off. We're both grunting as we grapple for the weapon. Her hand wraps around my wrist, shoving it down to my stomach as her legs come up and strangle my neck. She flips us over as she constricts her thighs.

"Thorn..." I see her name, releasing my grip on her armed hand.

She releases me from her hold and stands as I gasp for breath. "Take me out before hopping on top, investigator." She breathes out, her footsteps wandering away from me. "I'll see you around, Hale." Blackthorn smiles, her walk turning into a run.

I sit up, reaching for my knife and throw it, the blade only grazing her right leg. She stumbles from the pain and looks back towards me with a glare.

"I was gonna let you live, you prick." She hisses, switching her gun to her left hand. A glimmer catching my eye.

Is that?

Blackthorn raises the firearm, but her determination shifts to confusion, her brows knitting together as she glances at the Shadow Harmony.

"Take that off!" I scream, scrambling to my feet and rushing for her.

A red glow consumes my vision, a pulse hitting my chest.

THE MELDING

Investigator Adrian Hale

I groan, sitting up. My head spins and it takes a moment before I can get my eyes to focus. Blackthorn laying on the ground, but her hand.

"You idiot..." I mutter, shifting to my knees as I try to stand.

She touched it, worse she put the damn thing on. Did she even do her research on what she was grabbing? They locked it away for a reason. It's semi-sentient, aware of its users' needs. That by itself isn't what makes it dangerous, it's how it fulfils those needs. Blackthorn shifts a bit, lifting her arm upward, a soft reddish glow shimmering around the metallic surface. It's melded with her, which makes this a much bigger problem.

"Thorn!" I shout, forcing myself to my feet as I stumble my way towards her.

Seraphina 'Blackthorn' Wellington

My heartbeat is in my ears, my eyes staring at the fingerless gauntlet welded to my hand. I open my mouth to scream, but I hear him shout my name. With every shimmer of the light, I feel a pulse that isn't my own. Like it wants to take over for my heartbeat. I reach up with my other hand, my fingers ripping at my skin to pry this thing off of me.

"Get off!" I yell, the sides of my face now feeling damp. My efforts failing.

Hale kneels down next to me, grabbing my wrists. My reflexes bring my foot up, shoving him away from me, the momentum allowing me to do a back roll over. I stand, losing my balance from my vision shaking.

"Back off, Hale." I warn, raising my hand up.

I don't know what this thing is doing to me, but there's a chance he doesn't know either. Like I always say, fear is a great deterrent.

He stands, his hands raised and eyes wide. "Thorn, that thing is dangerous. You need to calm down before you activate it."

"Just shut up!" I shout at him, taking a few steps back.

The soft glow intensifies, and I lower my hand, its pulse quickening.

"Breathe Sera." I look back up to meet his eyes.

I could bet anything that if I looked in the mirror, I wouldn't recognise the person standing in front of it. My breathing is heavy. I taste the salty tears on my tongue and feel my lip trembling. I don't want to die.

"Listen to me, the artefact can feel your distress. For both of our sakes, just listen to me. I swear all I want to do at this moment is help you." His words come out slow. I can tell that he's trying to control the situation, but I can see him shaking. He is just as scared of whatever this thing really is or does.

The city's rhythmic beating shifts. The music, and hum of traffic stops. There's screaming, screeching of tires. Glass breaking.

"Sera, calm down!" He shouts sternly. A red hue illuminating his face.

I glance down the gauntlet now sparking with electrical currents. "I, I don't know what's happening." The words tumble out of my mouth.

The screams grow louder, no closer.

"Hale, what is this thing doing?" I ask, taking a step back.

I don't think this is worth that half a million anymore.

Hale's eyes widen, and he dives towards my gun. My jaw tightens, and I close my eyes.

This is it. I can't counter this. I failed. I actually failed.

The gun fires off three times, and I clench my stomach, waiting for the impact but it doesn't come, but the smell of sulphur does. I open my eyes to see something I only ever saw on the news. Boiled flesh, bits of fur or hair coming out in strange patches.

A monstrosity.

Hale exhales, his breaths uneven. He drops the gun and looks up at me. "Please, calm down." He whispers. "You're out of bullets."

I drop to my knees and look down at my hand, the intensity of the pulse and the glow now soft and subtle. This doesn't control the barrier to keep them out.

It controls them.

JOE PROSIT

Science Fiction Author

Author Joe Prosit

JOE PROSIT is an independent author living and writing in Brainerd, Minnesota. He has written several short stories that are available across the internet and in the anthology "Machines Monsters and Maniacs. His debut novel was *Bad Brains* and he has more sci-fi, horror, and psycho fiction is coming all the time. Learn more at: **www.joeprosit.com/**

Chapter Six
Everything On Three
By: Joe Prosit

T AKE A STRAW AND stick it through your skull. Probe around a little bit. Just until you hit the right nerve. The right memory. A good memory. A great memory. Then suck it out and plop it onto a scale. How much does it weigh? How much is it worth? Not just to you, but also to a whole slew of hypothetical buyers? How much would some other rememberer pay for experiencing a slice of your life? How much would you pay for a moment of a stranger's? How would you know if you're getting a fair deal before you lay down your hard-earned money?

You need a guy like Arnie.

Here's how the market works. The extraction is cleaner, less intrusive than physically sucking memories out with a straw. It's digitized, uninstalled, downloaded, and deleted from your mind as easy as an email. Then it's examined and appraised and encoded by a guy like Arnie. Once memories are financially quantified per current market values, they are traded, bartered, bet, and bought every day. And in a place as dismal as Cobalt City on Asteroid 138 of the Kuiper Belt? Memories are the hottest commodities on the market. The black market, that is. It doesn't mean trade is limited to such places. Hell, I even heard there's a whole hospice ward full of old rich bastards on Titan who are kept perpetually alive by living other people's recollections.

Me? I'm just a man looking to get back what's mine. On a mission for a memory. A memory as tangible as a stone buried in a fist.

"Seventy five bits," Arnie tells me and he dumps the data card in the metal tray under the blaster-proof permaglass window.

"That's it?" I say. "Last week you promised me two hundred for this kind of schlock. Now you're telling me you can't do better than a hundred?"

"No," Arnie says. "I'm telling you it ain't worth more than seventy five."

"What happened to two hundred?"

"That was last week, Stones. Listen, I can't predict the market."

I've heard this sermon before, and I don't need to hear it again.

As he pontificates over his woes of being a no-good, low-down, out-side-the-law memory appraiser stuck on an asteroid four billion miles from Earth, I avert my gaze away from his red, rheumy eyes. His shop is two levels below the surface. Cobalt City is a six-level-deep place without a single lump of cobalt left after the veins had been mined out and the ore shipped off-rock. When the mining company abandoned the tunnels, the Syndicate moved in and financed a place for lowlifes like Arnie and me to live. Not a nice place. Not a clean place. Not a bright and sunny place. But a place.

"Last week this kind of stuff was all the rage," Arnie carries on. "Filth, sin, decadence. If you came to me last week with this memory, I could maybe give you two hundred. This week? Decadence is out. Wholesome childhood memories are in. Maybe next week it will be highlights of successful careers in business, or sports victories, or religious epiphanies. Get this. Six months back, it was deaths that were real big. Deaths! The last minutes of somebody's life, harvested after they died and sold to the market by surviving family members looking to turn a quick buck. Who wants to relive someone dying, huh? People are real sick, you know that?"

"And you slapped a price tag on it for them, didn't you?" I ask.

"Hey. I'm just providing a service," he says, hands up as if this is a stickup and I'm the robber.

"Only crook around here is you, Arnie. You know that?" I say and aim a finger at him as if it were a blaster. "If this wasn't already illegal, I'd report you myself."

"Yeah, but that's the rub now ain't it? None of this is legal, and as far as authorities go, I'm about the best you got, ain't I?" he says.

I say nothing back. What the hell is seventy five bits going to do for me?

"Ain't I?" Arnie demands I confirm his ever-so-important position in our ever-so-seedy situation.

"Yeah, Arnie. You're a real patron saint," I say, but don't give me a second to get in a word. "You know what I had to do to get this memory?"

"'Course I know. I just valued it for seventy five bits, didn't I?"

"Yeah, you did. Now thankfully, I don't remember what it was I did to create that memory. All I know is you said the more degrading, the more dehumanizing, the more debasing, the better. And I brought you what you asked for, didn't I?"

"Oh yeah," Arnie snickers. "It's real nasty stuff."

"I ain't never done this sort of thing before. I ain't that kind of person. But last week you told me two hundred and I needed two hundred so I went and did it and now here I am, with the goods. Come on, man. Help me out here."

Now he's the one averting his gaze, examining the ceiling's exposed infrastructure of wiring and pipes and conduits and air exchangers and purifiers constantly pumping away to give us what passes for breathable air in this rock.

Still looking away, he says, "Eighty five."

I slam my fist on the counter. The card rattles in the tray.

"That's the best I can do and I can't budge one more bit. And this remains between us!" Now his finger is the one pressed against the permaglass. Would have been stabbed up my nose if it wasn't there. "If certain people in this city found out I'm doing favors and over-appraising memories higher than market value... That could be real bad for me. Like real bad. You get me?"

"Yeah, Arnie," I say. "I get you."

Appeased, he turns his attention back to the data card in the tray between us. "Does Julie know you did this?"

"Nope. And now that it's out of my head, I won't have to remember to lie about it either," I say.

"Well, all the same, best I can do is eighty five. You want the deal or not?"

"Yeah, I want the deal," I say.

"Tell you what I can do. I'll stamp my appraisal on it free of charge," Arnie says and scoops the data card out of the steel tray. "Cause I know you're a stand-up guy and you never hassle me and I know you're in a tight spot. But that's as far as my favors go. If you want any more charity, well, good luck finding it in this town."

"Don't I know it," I say as he goes to work encoding my memory with his grading.

According to the Syndicate, that encoding guarantees this is the one and only true copy of the memory. See, how they manage the market is by keeping tabs on guys like Arnie and ensuring they play by the rules. And rule Number One is No Copies. Nonfungible, they call it. See, once a memory is extracted, it's extracted wholly and completely. Nothing left behind from which to make a copy. What I did to create the memory Arnie is currently encoding, I don't recall. Normally, I got this habit of writing down a summary of any memories I have long before I ever think about downloading them and selling them. Not this one. When this one is gone, it's gone for good. All I know is that I was real desperate and willing to do some unspeakable things just to make it. Arnie told me what would get a higher grade, nasty, despicable stuff, and so I went and lived it so other people can remember it. And maybe those things are fun to relive when it's somebody else's soul incurring the cost. Vicarious, like. But in the moment? Let's just say that I'm glad it's out of my head and locked away inside that data card.

"There ya go, my friend," Arnie says and dumps the card back into the tray. "Don't say I never did anything for ya."

"Never would," I say, snatch the card out of the tray, and walk out the door.

Walking through the grim streets of Cobalt City, I've never felt further from the memory I'm trying to get back. Rock under my boots. Rock beyond the storefronts. Rock over my head. No sun. No stars. No natural breeze. No soft sandy beaches, warm yellow sun, or salt-flavored breezes. Nothing to smell but that burnt flavor of churned-up asteroid debris, grease, old food, and that burnt hair smell of triple-filter recycled air.

Of course, things being what they are, I don't remember the memory I'm trying to get back. All I have to go on is what I jotted down in my notebook before downloading it, getting it appraised, and bringing it into the gambling house six levels down. But no words can recreate a part of your life. No matter how well they're written. And let's face it, I'm no poet laureate. After I lost it to pocket aces, all I have left of it is my scribbles on a sheet of paper.

Family vacation back on Earth. Summer of '89. Oceanside Beach. Swam. Laid out and got a sunburn. Hung out on the boardwalk at night. Met a girl there. Fireworks. First kiss on the pier after dark. Her name was Beth.

That's it. If I search my brain for what Beth looked like, the color of her eyes, the smell of her hair, if the breeze blowing off the Pacific was warm or cool, I draw a blank. No idea. Arnie valued the memory at two hundred and fifty bits and then I watched it disappear across the felt of a poker table. Gone forever. Nothing left but the gap in time where it once was.

It's not the only gap I have in my memories. Hell, I've traded and swapped so many data cards it's getting to the point that I don't remember which ones are actually mine and which ones used to belong to somebody else. See, I wasn't planning on losing that memory of the trip to Oceanside. Only bet it cause I had pocket kings. Who loses with pocket kings? Nah. I was planning on winning a whole passel of memories that weren't my own, most of which I was ready to cash in so I could pay the rent, get some food, and maybe score a bottle of something for me and my lady to share.

Over the course of my dealings, have there been a few memories I plugged in for myself to enjoy? To fill in some of the missing parts of my own history? Sure I have. After all, life ain't easy being a cobalt miner on an asteroid fresh out of cobalt. So yeah, there have been a few things that have bounced between my big ears that weren't rightly mine by nature. That day spent driving a Porsche 3312 on the Autobahn at almost two hundred miles per hour? I know that one ain't mine. That threesome on a Martian swingers resort I got for doing a job for the syndicate? Not mine either. Memories like that, they go for big money, so of course I wasn't able to hold onto them for long. But I jotted them down in my notebook all the same. Other, more mundane memories? Memories that I might have actually had a chance at doing during my miserable life? Memories that don't have much value except to me? I think most of those are mine. I know Oceanside is mine. I know Beth is mine. I know it.

And I'm going to get it back.

"Well, ain't that something?" I say to myself as I stroll through Cobalt City's entertainment district. As I live and breathe the recycled asteroid air, so help me if that isn't the man who stole my memory from me with a pair of aces. Yavrik. That son of a bitch.

He's smoking dreamflower on the balcony of an open-all-night dance club thumping music so loud I hear it three blocks coming. He's leaning on the rail, back to the street and butt to me, but I still recognize him. If I had any real luck, he'd tip over the side, pinwheel the whole way down, break his neck, and die in the street at my feet. No chance of that, unless someone gives him a nudge in the right direction, that is.

All the club's windows are open. The noise and strobing lights flood the street. Most people hustle by. I head for the bouncer at the door and pay the cover.

The interior has got to be the hottest place on this whole stinking rock. Hundreds of bodies are packed in here, mashing against each other and creating more heat by friction. The whole joint reeks like the repulsive combination of a gym, a candy store, and a distillery. Yavrik is on the second floor. I fight my way through the dancing crowd, pushing and shoving through the dancers who are too taken by the dreamflower to know I'm even there. Eventually, I find a spiral staircase near the back and circle my way up. The second floor is just as full as the first and I can only make my way to the balcony with a liberal application of elbows, knees, and boots. By the time I'm across the room, I'm soaked with sweat and deaf from the drumbeat.

Stepping out onto the balcony cuts the temperature by twenty degrees, easy. The roar of the music softens too. Same goes for the smells. The day-old-fart stench of the recyclers is a welcome relief. The only unpleasant thing about being out here rather than in there is Yavrik.

"Stones!" he calls my name as soon as I'm clear of the crowd.

He has a heavyweight next to him who is undoubtedly packing a blaster. So much for sneaking up on Yavrik and dumping him over the railing. That's fine. Although that's what I want to do with every fiber of my body, even I ain't so dense as to not know when to go full agro and when to use a little finesse.

"Yavrik, funny seeing you again so soon," I say, only loud enough to be heard over the bass, so a decibel below screaming.

"Funny seeing you here. You don't seem like the partying type," he half-speaks half-screams back.

I step closer, around some stools. What I have to say, I prefer not to yell it through the streets. The big fella next to him steps closer too.

"Listen. Yavrik. You still have that data card?" I say, hoping to avoid any incriminating vocabulary. Even Cobalt City has its cops, and they're never too shy to thump your head for ya if they catch you mixed up in anything vaguely illegal.

"The memory? The one I won from ya with a pair of pocket rockets?" Yavrik says.

So much for discretion.

"How could I forget? Won it fair and square too," he reminds me.

"Yeah. Yeah, I know you did. But I got something you might like better," I say and pull my newly encoded data card from a jacket pocket.

Yavrik takes one glance at it and sees Arnie's stamp on the case. "Eighty five? Man, you know what I won from you is graded way higher than eighty five measly bits."

"Yeah, I know. But what I gave you... it's nostalgia bait. Boring, wholesome stuff. It won't mean nothing to you. But this?" I flag the card in front of his nose. "This is exactly the kind of stuff I know you like. Real sleazy. Real greasy. Right up your alley."

He chokes on an inhale of dreamflower and hacks the acidic smoke back in my face. "You know me, Stones! Got me pinned; that's for damn sure. Let me see what you got."

I let him hold the data card, enough for him to read the appraisal stamp, but I don't let it go. Trust is as short as a hair measured sideways. The stamp will give him a rough idea of what's inside. Location. Genre. Event summary. Duration. That's all he needs.

"Damn, Stones," he says. "You really did that?"

I nod. "Yeah, but it will feel like you doing it when you download it."

"You sick son of a bitch! You really stepped out of your comfort zone for this one, huh?" Yavrik laughs.

"Let's just say I had a certain customer in mind when I made it," I say. Now, please take it off my hands and give me back what's mine, I think but don't say.

"Does your lady friend know about this?" he asks. "What's her name again? Judy, is it?"

"No. And once you take it, she won't ever know about it," I say, intentionally not correcting him. "Are you ready to make a deal or what?"

"Okay. Okay. But with a stamp like that, you gotta sweeten the pot a little. Throw in a hundred bits and this is all yours." He pulls a data card from his pocket. On Arnie's stamp, it reads *Earth. Nostalgia. Childhood vacation w/ First Kiss. Forty Eight Hours.* My data card. My memory. My only hope to ever relive that perfect night on the Oceanside Pier with... I search for her name and only remember it from writing it down in my notebook... Beth.

"Yav, I don't have a hundred bits," I tell him. No lie there. "Let me give you fifty now and I'll owe ya the rest."

"No gold, no goods, my man. Hit me with that nasty stuff you got there and the full hundo and I'll hand her over. Otherwise, door's that way, pal," Yavrik says.

"Yav, come on. How long have we known each other? Float me fifty. That's all I'm asking," I say.

"And maybe you ain't heard me," Yavrik says. And like a dog at the heel, his big friend takes another step, this one putting himself between me and Yavrik. He fills up the space quite effectively. "Either out the front door or..." Yav's eyes drift over the railing as if I haven't noticed that exit routine from the beginning.

"I'll take the stairs if you don't mind."

Julie and I, we have an apartment about a mile from the club and one level deeper. Three levels down. Not Syndicate territory, but not far from it. It's a five by five meter cube in which Julie and I have packed all our possessions and keep all our peace. It's a haven from the rest of Cobalt City. Out there, the wild dogs run in droves. In here, we're doves cooing in our quiet coop. When I come through the door, she's lying on our bed like an angel on a cloud. I shut the door behind me. I don't want to share this view with anyone.

With a tap of a button, she clicks the screen off. Whatever she'd been watching is gone and our domicile abides in the soft noises of the asteroid's ever-churning infrastructure. And the way she looks at me, her body stretched out as it is, she could be a work of art. She's not posing for a sculptor's masterwork or anything. All the same, she's Athena, Aphrodite, and Artemis all rolled into one. Only draped in half a blanket, her shorts, and a cut-off tank top, I savor the curves of her skin as if they're polished marble. Her eyes flash like diamonds. Her bored face that turns into a smile when she sees me melts my problems like wax under a candle's flame. If I have had any luck in life, it's here, far away from any poker table. She pats the empty spot of the mattress next to her, not saying a word.

My boots kick off and thump against the wall. My jacket and clothes fall to the floor as I make my way to her. Falling into bed feels soft, like falling into a dream. Her lips feel like a touch of sunshine warming the corner of my mouth. When she scootches her body next to mine, I'm cocooned in her warmth. On our backs, our eyes peer upward.

There's an old maintenance shaft directly above our bed. The view used to be clogged with fans and motors and vents, but I cleared all that out two years ago when we moved in together. Now we have a clear view, all the way up to the surface, where a permaglass panel is all that keeps us from the void of space. Beyond that panel, all the stars hang in their places in the heavens. The vast infinity. The fireflies that drew us away from the safety of Earth all the way out here to the Kuiper Belt all those years ago. The promise of wealth and riches and adventure. Funny, how all we want now is each other.

"Long day?" I ask her.

"Pulled a double shift at Blondie's," she says. Blondie's is a beer and booze hall on the surface and the only reason the two of us aren't in a debter's prison right now. "You?" she asks.

"Long week," I say.

"Where were you two nights ago, anyway?" she asks.

"Don't remember," I say, because not knowing and not remembering are two different things.

"You saw Arnie again, didn't you?" she asks.

Any other woman, I would have lied. Anyone else asks, and I'll give them the answer they want to hear. But Julie, she has ways of getting me to lower my dukes.

"I was trying to make some extra bits. And now? Well, there's this memory from when I was a kid. We took this family trip to Earth. Swam in the ocean. I flirted with girls on the boardwalk. That sort of thing. And now... I need it back. It's like there's a part of me that made me who I am that's just missing. It's a part of who I am. No different than if I'd lost a finger or a foot."

"Stoney," she chastises me, and for good reason. I should have never gotten tied up in the market to begin with, and she is my best reminder of that. "You promised me you were done with all that. That you wouldn't see Arnie anymore."

"Don't blame Arnie. Besides, we needed the money," I say. "Look, I don't like it any more than you do. But with all the mining gone, there's no work around here. We gotta eat, don't we?"

"We can scrap by. I got a twenty bit tip today. That will get us some foot we can make last. And there's still plenty of other business, legit business being done on this rock. If you look for it, I know you can find a decent job that won't get you mixed up with anything the Syndicate touches."

"I'm sorry. I wish I could take it back, believe me. What can I say? I was hungry. And I knew you were hungry too and I had nothing left but what was in my head. So..."

"So, you won't do it again?" she asks.

"Sure. Never again," I say. "Just as soon as I get back what I lost."

"Stoney!"

"I swear! One more deal and then I'm out," I say.

"How do you know that memory is even yours?" she says. "You've had so many installed and extracted from that head of yours—"

"I know this one is mine," I say. "It shaped my life, Julie. My personality. My soul. There's only so much you can take away from a person and expect them to stay the same. Without that memory, I feel less grounded, less whole, less moral, less *me*. I mean, what are we without our memories?"

"That's why you should have never gone to him," Julie says. "You know there are counterfeits out there, right? Copies? Forgeries? I told you Arnie was trouble from the start."

"It's not Arnie I'm worried about; it's the son of a bitch that has my youth on a data card inside his filthy jacket pocket," I say. "But I got a plan. Just gotta play the market, wait for the price to drop, and get it back. No big thing."

"Stoney," Julie sighs.

"That's all there is to it, Jules," I say. "I gotta get this one back, and then I'm done. I promise."

A handful of seconds tick by. We map the rotation of the asteroid by the motion of the stars beyond the maintenance shaft. I listen to her breath. I hate myself for arguing with her. She doesn't deserve my frustrations and problems. She deserves better than that. She deserves better than me.

"Can I help you feel better?" she asks and runs her hand over my chest.

"Always," I say.

What follows isn't sex. Not the common, biological, or pornographic thing. No. We make love under the stars. My view alternates between her twinkling eyes above me and the dusting of diamonds beyond the maintenance shaft. Things of beauty, those glittering gems, but the pair outshine the plentitude as if all the rest of the universe has been swallowed up by a black hole.

Here, underneath her, everything is okay again. Everything is as it should be. Everything is perfect. Even if all my other life experiences fall into the black hole of forgetfulness along with all the stars, I still have this.

Afterwards, when we're both in the no-man's land between day and dreams, she whispers in my ear, "Stoney?"

"Yeah," I whisper back.

"The past is the past. We're our future," she says.

"You're right, babe. You're always right."

"So just let it go," she says, as if it's the easiest solution ever spoken. As easy as slipping into dreams in her arms.

"Okay," I promise. "I'll let it go."

I'm tempted to jot down a summation of this night in my little notebook resting there on the nightstand. I know what I would write too, as insufficient as it would be: *Making love in our bed. The stars shining down the narrow maintenance shaft. My whole life in a five by five meter cube. All my heart contained in a woman shorter than two meters tall. Her name is Julie.* But I don't, because I wouldn't trade this away for all the bits in the Belt. The notebook stays untouched. The memory stays inside my head.

Over the course of the next two weeks, I stay away from Arnie. And Yavrik. And the casinos. Instead, I find a temporary gig making deliveries. All through the crust, up to the surface, even down to the sixth level where the Syndicate runs the appraisers and the dealers. But I keep my distance from anything illegal. Julie was right about that, there is still honest work to be found on this rock if you look in the right places.

On one trip up to the surface, I even find the permaglass panel above our maintenance shaft. With a little work, most of the dust and grime comes right off.

We buy groceries. A bottle of bathtub gin even. We celebrate. We spend more time in our bed. The stars shine a little brighter through the cleaned-up panel. Things are good.

Still, I can't shake that nagging feeling of something missing. It's like that feeling you get when you set something down, just for a second, and someone else picks it up before you have a chance to notice. Like you forgot something, but you can't remember for the life of you what it is you forgot. Like walking down the steps at night and thinking you've reached the bottom, just for your foot to fall another step further down.

I took my notebook and buried it deep in a drawer of my nightstand. Better to focus on the present. Better to focus on what I have and hold onto that. Like Julie said, the past is the past. We're our future. See, you never really understand how much you've gained until you've experienced loss.

And then, on a day like all the ones before it, the address for Arnie's shop appears on my list of deliveries. As temporary as this position is, I don't have the option to refuse to make the stop. If I don't follow the list, they'd just move on to the next ex-miner lowlife who will. So I grit my teeth and make my way back along an all too familiar path.

When I shoulder open the door, I don't look up from the chipped tile floor. Figure all I have to do is set the package on his desk and be on my way. Don't have to say a word. Keep it quick, simple, and pure. Two steps through the door, my plan starts to crumble.

"Stones, is that you?" Arnie calls through the permaglass barrier. "Where the hell you been, man?"

Okay. Fine. So there's no getting out of here without at least speaking to the man. I can still do this. Just make the delivery and get out. Just like all the rest. Doesn't have to lead to anything else.

"How's it going, Arnie?" I say over my jacket collar. "Got a package for you. Then I gotta be on my way."

"Sure, sure. Set it down other there. What have you been up to man? You know, decadence is back up! I can probably re-appraise that memory you brought in last we talked. Give you that two hundred you were looking for even."

"Sold it," I say, because I would have given that data card away. And if I couldn't find anyone to take it, I would have incinerated it in a blast furnace rather than hang on to it.

"Shame. Damn shame," he says. "Death is up again. Birth is up too. Guess people want the whole soup-to-nuts nowadays."

"You have a strange business, Arnie," I say. "Hey, I'd love to stay and chat, but they got me on a timer with these deliveries. Gotta get the next package ten kilometers across the surface and I got... twenty minutes to do it."

"Sure. Of course. I never want to be the guy standing between a man and his money," Arnie says. "But, hey. Before you run off. Just one second."

"Time is money, Arnie. Even a second," I say, not knowing just how costly one might be.

"Real quick, real quick," he says and waves me closer to that grimy, blaster-proof window. "That memory you lost. The one of you back on Earth. On the beach."

I shake my head and shift toward the door. This is a game he's playing. He's always playing a game, working an angle, hustling a trick.

"I know where you can find it," he says. "Childhood memories are down right now. Bet even you can afford it at current market rates."

"Yeah?" I say, knowing I should keep walking, but I did have some bits bouncing around in my pocket now that I was working again.

"I mean, it only came down a little," Arnie shrugs. "One of my competitors appraised it for two hundred even at a casino six levels down."

"At even two hundred, huh?" I say.

"Yeah. They got it as a pay-out prize for baccarat," he says.

"Baccarat," I say. I know the game. Know it well. Know all the strategies and the numbers behind them. And I'm damn good with them too. Of all the ways you can play against the house, baccarat has the best odds.

"Maybe the beach back on Earth, all those billions of miles from here, maybe it ain't so far away after all," Arnie says. "Course, you'll need some collateral to get yourself a seat at the table. You got anything good on, ya?"

"Nah, man. I told you, I'm out of the game. Me and the market are done," I tell him.

"That's a shame. Real shame. Besides Death and Birth, you know what else is up this week?" he says.

"Trust me, I got nothing you want. Besides, I already told you, I'm not interested. I'm out. I lost too much already."

"Ah, but what if you had it all back? Just ask me. Ask me what the market has an appetite for this week. I can only guarantee a favorable appraisal today. Might not be the same tomorrow or the next day or next week."

"I don't need it. It was good seeing ya, Arnie, but I got this delivery," I say and head toward the door. "See ya next time around."

"It's Romance," he calls after me.

My boots scuff to a stop in front of the door. Without turning around, I ask over my shoulder, "What do you mean, 'romance'?"

"You know. Romance! Hugs and kisses and all that bull. Old fashion falling in love. Look around ya, bub. If there's one commodity that's in short supply around here, it's love," Arnie says. "But you wouldn't happen to have any of that bouncing around between those two low-hanging ears of yours, wouldja?"

"You said it's in a baccarat pot?" I say.

"Beat the dealer and win a prize! I mean, I ain't check it myself, but you can go have a look. That is if they let you in the door. Only high rollers allowed in this place. My competitor's stamp will be covering the stamp from when you had me value it, but you'll still be able to check the serial number. Make sure it's yours," he says.

"Six levels down. A lot of counterfeits that far from the surface," I say. Telling him? Telling myself?

"I can only vouch for my own work, of course. Can't speak for my competitors," he says. "If you do have something, something the market might be interested in, I can give you a fair value. We're friends, you and I, remember? Remember I did that thing for you? And now you've been holding out on me. What kind of friendship is that?"

"We were never friends, Arnie," I turn to him and say.

"Funny, you saying that after I've stuck my neck out for you. Funnier still seeing as how I can still do you this one more favor."

"You know how much that memory means to me," I say as I come back to that blaster-proof window. "Never mind what the market says it's worth."

"So you've said. And I'm telling you, right now, it's a buyer's market for childhood recollections. And a seller's market for romance. Forget all that decadence stuff we've dealt with before. This is the good stuff," he says. "I wouldn't ask you to do any of that stuff again. Never asked you in the first place. It'd be a shame if something as depraved as what's in this data card ever came to light," Arnie says and places a data card down on the counter behind the permaglass.

"Is that what I think it is?" I say.

"Yep. Can't move the damn thing though. Nobody is into this kind of smut. Not today anyway. Not unless I present it to a certain interested party," he says.

"An interested party like me?" I ask.

"You... or maybe a certain lady currently working for tips at Blondie's Tavern," he says.

Before I can think, my fist slams into the barrier in front of his face. It wobbles in its sill, but of course doesn't break. Some of the bones in my hand maybe, but not the permaglass. He's lucky it's there.

"Give it to me," I say.

"What do you want this ol' thing for?" he says.

"So I can destroy it. You said it yourself, it's worthless. Give it to me and–"

"And?" he leads me.

"And I'll let you in on what I got," I say.

"Fifty bits," he says. "I gotta charge you this time. After doing you that favor last time. Fifty bits and I'll throw in this old data card along with the appraisal for a new one. A deal any better than that and I'll have the syndicate coming down on my head and shoulders. This is a friend deal. 'Cause we are friends, Stoney. You and I. I'm looking out for ya, see? Wouldn't want nothing bad to come between you and your lady friend, now would we?"

"And you swear my memory is where you say it is? Six levels down, in a baccarat pot?" My childhood. My innocence. My morality. My purity. A touchpoint of my youth that made me who I am today. All those things I want to tell him, explain to him how off-base his market-value appraisals are. But I don't. Cause that's not how deals are made. Never let on how valuable the thing is you're trying to get your hands on. Take advantage of the market. Buy when the price is down. Sell when it's high. Simple as that.

I just need enough collateral to get me in the door. I can use the smut data card for the bet.

"Would I lie to you?" Arnie says and his blurry, red eyes lock with mine.

Six levels down, the filth of our little asteroid society only gets thicker. Like the bottom deck of a ship, it's all rats down here. Crooked appraisers. Loan sharks. Syndicate goons. Dens lined with Dreamflower addicts. Cat houses. I wish I could say I've never set foot this far from the surface, but my feet know the way to the casino like a horse bringing a drunk cowboy back to the ranch. I flash a data card at the doorman to let him know I can sit with the big rollers as much as anyone else. He unclips the velvet rope. The high-stakes prize-pot baccarat tables are through the main lobby and all the way to the right. And yeah, there on display for everyone to envy over is a rack of data cards behind permaglass, each labeled with a number one through ten. Third from the right is one with an appraisal stamp that reads: *Earth. Nostalgia. Childhood vacation w/ First Kiss. Forty Eight Hours.* The stamp with the new grade and value almost entirely covers Arnie's stamp underneath it. And the serial number. It's my memory alright. Goddamn right it's mine. Always has been. Should have never let it out of my head from the start. I know that now.

I find a table with just a dealer and one other player. My newly appraised data card thumps heavy against the felt. "I'm playing for Number Three. Put it all on Number Three."

"Number Three, huh?" the player to my left says.

Looking over, I see it's Yavrik. "It's a good one," he says, and he would know. Of all people, he would know. "And you better believe it's what I'm looking to get back too."

Looking at that stupid painted-on smile of his, I'd bet all the bits in the Belt to wipe it clean off his face. I brought two data cards into this place. One of which had an appraisal of just twenty five bits. As for the data card resting on the felt, it's worth a full two hundo and reads *Asteroid 138 of Kuiper Belt, Romance, True Love Under the Stars, Two Years Intermittently.*

In my jacket pocket is a slip of paper I wrote on before downloading my memories onto the data card. It doesn't say much. Just two short sentences:

Her name is Julie. Don't lose her.

Funny thing is, I don't even know anybody by the name.

IVY RU

Up And Coming Horror Author

Author Ivy Ru

IVY RU has been sharing stories from a very early age and *Otherworldly* is her debut publication! Some of her first works consist of tales of her adventures with her imaginary sister Sinnamon, but she's also published a short story in a young author anthology and co-written a Dungeons & Dragons adventure with her dad. When she's not at school or the keyboard, Ivy spends her time playing percussion, harp, and piano and practicing many forms of dance. Ivy loves spending time with her cats and aspires to become a full-time author.

CHAPTER SEVEN
The Call From Below

By: Ivy Ru

I T WAS 8:00 A.M. when I received the call.

It was 8:00 A.M. when my life changed forever.

Everything started normally. I had been called to work early. We had scheduled routine maintenance on the NanoTech computers and I needed to ensure that all of Mr. Anderson's files were intact. I loved coming in early to Nanotech. Lin City was still dark, and the speakers that usually emitted sounds of birds now filled the air with the calming chirp of crickets. The city was still, and the smell of street-cleaning solution filled the air with the scent of imitation lemon.

I arrived at the building while the night cleaning crew was leaving, and I walked to my office in silence. I brushed my hand against the smooth marble railing as I climbed the plush stairs, taking in the grandeur of the building. It had magnificent architecture combined with sleek materials—a masterpiece. Whenever I entered Nanotech, I knew it was exactly where I belonged.

My office was as I had left it the day before, with shining white floors and crystal-clear windows that stretched the entire height of the room. I had suggested adding some color to the room. My request had been denied. Not good for productivity. Mr. Anderson was very particular about his suite and preferred when the cleaning crew avoided his office or adjacent rooms for fear of them misplacing a tablet that had been left out. I always thought this was strange because I never left a tablet out, but I also never argued.

I began my work, double and triple checking that each and every one of Mr. Anderson's files was in the right place. Usually, I could become completely engrossed in my work, but that day, I felt *off.* With a quick scan of the room, I realized that nothing was physically out of place. It was something in the air.

That's when I got the call.

The line number looked like it had originated from a lower level of the city, but it was easy to mistake different levels' numbers at a quick glance. I opened the call quickly and spoke into my earpiece, you should never leave someone on the other line for too long; that was one the first things Mr. Anderson had ever taught me.

"Hello! This is Ms. Stao at Nanotech Incorporated, how may I assist you?" I asked.

The caller breathed loudly, something I detested.

"Hello?" I spoke again, louder this time.

"Have you seen the belly of the beast?"

The silence following the question was like a herd of elephants. The caller sounded like they would continue, but I wouldn't let them. I couldn't let them. I had gotten strange calls before, but none that made my stomach drop like this one had.

"Thank you for your call, have a pleasant day." I said as calmly as I could.

I had known fake calls were part of the job description, but they still concerned me whenever the office received one. Every time I got a call like this, it was hard to get back to work; it felt like someone was watching me. Of course, someone was watching me, there were security cameras everywhere.

I left my office and walked around the perimeter of Nanotech to calm my mind. The silence of the city and the blue skies of the upper levels were always able to comfort me when I was stressed about work, I could actually hear myself think outside, without the quiet buzz of technology in my office. I don't know how I would ever think if I had to listen to even more noise all day.

When Nanotech moved its headquarters to Lin City, the company made some changes. All of the residents of the upper city, and some of the middle levels, were required to wrap all household appliances with a thick, sound-dampening foam that absorbed any sound they made. Lights in the lower city and factories were swapped for blue. The lack of sunlight in the lower levels made it so the blue lights obscured almost every color. Noiseless trams had been installed throughout the upper city, and any transportation other than foot traffic was made impossible by the web of catwalks and scaffolding in the rest of the city.

Those changes were made seventy-three years ago, and now the city is even more polished. It has been made a pinnacle for the rest of the world. I am part of that pinnacle.

I returned to my office after walking to find that Mr. Anderson had already begun working in his suite, and a stack of new files was waiting for me. Usually, I was happy to have work waiting for me, I could dive in and forget about the outside world for a few hours. Instead, I tracked the origin of the call through my console. I suppose someone could blame something like this on human curiosity, but the tug in my gut felt stronger than human nature. I was right that it had been a lower city number and an old one at that. Numbers tied to a specific place were only issued in special cases. I switched the address coordinates to my datapad and walked out of the building. Everyone trusted that I was going somewhere important, and they didn't try to stop me.

My parents made it easy for me to go wherever I wanted. My father had worked closely with Mr. Anderson when they were younger. They were the reason that NanoTech was where it is today. That was why, when I lost my vision as a child, I received an intraocular implant and nanobot treatments. Once I was old enough to work, Mr. Anderson was more than happy to hire me as his assistant. No one had questioned me before I began working, and they were even less likely to now.

I walked past the tram station and arrived at a large white gate, the entrance to the lower sections of the city. You didn't need your identification to get into the lower levels, you only needed it to get back up.

I began my trek down the cascading waterfall of sidewalks, passing other upper city citizens there on business, and some lower city workers on their mandatory breaks. My parents had told me that they got too many breaks, if I was able to work all day surely they were as well, right? I finally reached the coordinates in the seventh ring of the city. There was no light except for the blue bulbs on every store and house porch. The address led me to a blue-washed convenience store with a blue OPEN sign illuminating the front step. A single-use datapad was next to the front step, and the start-up screen had my name on it.

I looked around the street and saw workers quickly approaching with clear plastic lunch bags, so I stashed the tablet in my jacket. I walked back to the upper city, resisting the urge to run when I saw someone look in my direction. Some may say I was over-cautious, but I was terrified of being caught with an unauthorized datapad. When I arrived in the upper city I scanned my ID badge and entered my apartment.

I opened the tablet at my desk, and when it asked for a fingerprint, it recognized mine as the owner.

> Hello Aria, we hope this message finds you well. cahoNnet nad-pecrroIto is not what it seems. You must find the belly of the beast. The safety of Lin City rests in your hands alone. Level 2 299.

The caller's phrase, "the belly of the beast," rang in my head from my previous encounter with the term. I recognized the last part of the message as an address, one that was on a lower level than I had ever been.

There were a total of twelve levels in the city. I had gone down to level seven today when I was tracking the call, and that was the lowest I had ever explored. Most people on level seven worked as low-level managers who traveled around the city, or people of my station visiting for meetings. Level two was different. Those living on level two were factory workers and manual laborers. Many of them had never seen the sun, and would never see the sun.

Pictures of the lower levels weren't often shown to those in the upper city, so I had never even seen what it was like. I had heard about it, and that reaffirmed my action of never going. But it looked like I would need to go now if I ever wanted to find out what was happening.

The next day, I did just that.

I woke up earlier than normal and called in sick to work. I swapped my blue uniform for common clothing and ate a breakfast of nutrient packs before leaving my apartment. The view of the sky from the twelfth level was still black and the lights from the lower city shone up through cracks in the various platforms. I found a recycling unit and wiped the datapad I had found on seven, leaving it to be used for another, less creepy purpose. I left the upper city by way of a vertical tram, I couldn't risk anyone seeing me walk down. The tram only traveled to level five, and I had to walk the rest of the way. I kept my head covered with my dark coat whenever I passed someone, which in hindsight, probably made me look more suspicious than I intended.

I held my personal datapad in my hand and looked for the address on every door on level two. The smell was disturbing, and I wanted to go back to my cozy apartment as fast as I could. I heard a sound and stopped. Only for a second, but it was long enough. A figure sat huddled on the steps of a run-down house, staring at me with large, tear-filled eyes.

I turned back toward the street and walked faster. I couldn't stop for anyone, no matter what. My parents always told me I shouldn't feel sorry for those on lower levels. If they had worked harder they would be successful like we were. Their words didn't stop the twinge of guilt I felt whenever I saw someone asleep on the corner or digging in the collectors for food.

I had expected the people on levels as low as this to be aggressive and dangerous, but I guessed the blue light had prevented that. The lights had been installed to keep people calm and focused. Nanotech wanted their workers to be productive, but these people just looked dejected and sleep-deprived.

When I found 299, I sighed in relief. It was another convenience store, the same company as before. I looked around but found no datapad this time, only another blue sign that read OPEN. With no better ideas, I stepped inside. The lights gave everything a blue tone, and the labels on packaged meals were barely legible.

I took a lap around the store, looking for hidden signs as I reread the message from my pad.

cahoNnet nadpecrrolto

I had looked everywhere in the store, scanned every shelf, and found nothing. I clenched my fist in frustration and grabbed a can off a nearby shelf, ready to throw it at the concrete floor. But I stopped.

In my hand I held a can that read; "cahoNnet nadpecrrolto The Best Shelf Fruit for You and Me!" I twisted the can in my hand.

The can looked like all the others on the shelf, a dark blue package with a stylized picture of tropical fruit in bold colors, But the name of the product had been edited on this one. I shoved the can in my bag and left the store, ignoring the calls of the shop-runner. I couldn't let anyone see this can.

I ran up through the city and found refuge behind a meal station on level five. I pulled the package out of my bag and opened it like an animal, ignoring the plastic that cut my hands. Inside the mangled package was a small chip the size of a pea. I inspected the chip between my fingers. It was metal, covered with intricately placed gold wires.

I shook the rest of the contents of the package out into my hand, and besides a few pieces of dry fruit, there was a note written on plain paper. Paper was expensive in the city, as almost everyone used datapads when they needed to write anything. The note only had two words.

"Mari Nev"

It was a name, and I knew who it belonged to. Mari Nev had worked as a doctor in the lower levels of Lin City before being charged with performing illegal cosmetic surgeries. Turning people into animal-like creatures and putting patients under his knife to perform unimaginable experiments. And I needed to find him.

I grabbed a booth in an automated diner and began my search, starting with broad terms on my datapad. I found hundreds of news and tabloid pieces about the doctor's various scandals, court cases, and victims. It seemed like journalists had been tripping over themselves to find the location of his next secret lab or photographs of his experiments. When I finally found an article about his capture, I was surprised. Mari Nev had not been executed like most dangerous criminals were, he was still in Lin City.

I stayed overnight on the seventh level. It was too likely to see someone I knew any higher. I called Nanotech employee security to inform them that I would be out sick for a second day, and though they sounded skeptical they were smart enough not to question me. I knew it would be dangerous for my parents if I were caught outside of work, and it was better if I pretended I couldn't go at all.

Dr. Nev had been imprisoned on the lowest level of the city, the one reserved for criminals alone. You needed incredibly high clearance codes to access the level. Lucky for me, being the Executive Assistant to the highest-ranking official of Nanotech came with some perks.

I told the guards at the front gate that Mr. Anderson required certain information about a prisoner, and that I was sent to collect it personally. I expected a barrage of questions, but with a flash of my Nanotech ID, a guard led me into the city's highest security prison.

Dr. Nev was kept in a dark corner of the vast building, at the end of a long line of cells made by green electric fields. Other prisoners looked at me as I passed, some begged for food only to be met by an electric shock from the walls of their cell.

The guard accompanying me gestured to Dr. Nev's cell. On one side of the field, there was a fingerprint pad and a cell number. I could barely see the doctor until I stood directly in front of the door.

"I need to speak privately with Dr. Nev. I will let you know if I require assistance." The guard looked at me for a moment before walking back towards the entrance to the hall. I turned to the doctor.

"Dr. Nev," I pulled the chip out from my pocket. "Do you know what this is?"

The electric field shimmered as the man in the corner approached. He was thin, no doubt as a result of the prison diet, and stood hunched, with long white hair tied in braids and deeply wrinkled skin. A look of recognition darted through his eyes.

"Where did you get that?"

"Doctor, do you know what this is? My employer and I find this information extremely valuable."

The Doctor looked at me, stony eyes meeting mine.

"Yes, I know what it is. It's a storage chip for a B12 intraocular implant. The B12 model was only used for a few years before they locked me up here. What I don't know is why you have it."

I was confused, and it showed in my voice "I found it, and I think it was left for me to find. It was left next to a note with your name on it. why?"

"I'm the only doctor who knows the procedure and isn't currently employed with Nanotech, and If my suspicions are correct, I'm the one who made that chip."

I was surprised that someone outside of Nanotech had gotten their hands on this kind of advanced technology, but I had known Nev was skeevy since the first time I had read his name.

"How did you get Nanotech technology?" I asked.

The doctor laughed for an uncomfortably long time before answering. "You poor, naive girl. Nanotech is not the only intelligent group in the city. If you trust me, you will be able to see so much more. You will see the truth about it all."

"How can I see the information?" I asked, "If it's a data chip, there must be somewhere I can view it."

I was picturing something like a special datapad port, or a computer in the upper city. The truth was much more gruesome.

"The only way to view the information is to connect the data chip directly to the B12 implant. No shortcuts I'm afraid."

I turned away from the grinning doctor, "If, hypothetically, I did want the surgery, what would you want in exchange?"

"You get me out of here, and I'll do it. But I won't be coming back after we're done."

I called the guard back to the cell. "I am going to give you money now, and you are going to let this man go."

I showed the guard a transfer waiting to be confirmed from my funds on my datapad. His eyes lit up, but I could see hesitation in how his hand rested on his weapon.

"If you don't let this man walk out with me," I went on, "I may have to report an incident to my supervisor, Mr. Anderson."

The guard's eyes widened before he scrambled to the pin pad next to the cell, not even checking to see if the transfer had happened before scurrying away from me and the doctor. Some might say my method was too direct, but I didn't want to waste time with pleasantries.

The doctor stepped out of the cell, holding onto my arm for balance. He shook like a leaf in the wind, making my own legs unsteady. His pale, bony fingers wrapped around my wrist and I could feel his jagged fingernails cutting through my jacket. I held him up but his physical condition was worrying. I had read that he was incarcerated when he was fifty-three, and twenty years later he resembled a ninety-year-old.

"Are you positive you will be able to perform the procedure?" My voice wavered, but I quickly corrected it.

Mari Nev was not someone to whom you wanted to show fear.

"My legs may be weak but my hands are as steady as ever," he said. "I will perform the surgery."

Dr. Nev followed me from the building, guards watching us closely for every step we took. The only way out of level one was by armed escort, and as we made our way back to level two, the officers trailing us did nothing to prevent the stares I had predicted we would see. Nev had been incarcerated so long ago that he was nearly unrecognizable.

I rented a basement from a family on the sixth level, wanting to apologize for what would take place in their home. I stayed in the small living room to sleep and advised Dr. Nev to do the same, but when I woke only twenty minutes later, the doctor was walking through the basement door with bags full of medical equipment. The dining table was sterilized with a glowing device that shed light onto the entire room, and the doctor laid out a series of implements on a small tray next to the table. Dr. Nev donned a plastic mask and mismatched latex gloves. It was hard to tell behind the mask, but I could've sworn he was grinning as he wiggled his fingers into the gloves.

As I stood next to the table, a flood of anxiety rushed through me, what was I even doing? Was I going insane?

"What on the chip anyway? Why do I need to see it?"

The doctor held the chip to the light "If I am correct, this chip has sensitive and important information. I believe I know what organization left it for you to find." He spoke matter-of-factly, like I hadn't just helped him escape from prison, or that we weren't about to perform surgery on my eye.

"What organization?" I had never heard of any groups besides Nanotech having access to this kind of technology.

"With the information on this, you will find out soon enough."

I didn't trust Dr. Nev, but I did trust that whatever was on this chip would change everything.

"Let's do it."

I came to with Dr. Nev leaning over me wearing his surgical gear and giving me a thumbs up, a strange sight to see as you woke up from a medical procedure.

"The surgery was a success. Your implant should be receiving the data shortly."

I looked around and blinked spots from my eyes, "I'm not seeing anything-"

Text scrolled across my vision so quickly that I could barely read it. Pictures flashed in front of me. Pictures of myself, pictures of the different levels of the city, and some pictures of people I had never seen before. I explained everything to the doctor as fast as I could and he typed it all into my datapad. And then it was over. Just as fast as the information had appeared, it was gone.

I remembered the flash of information from when I had first received the implant, but it had just been codes and numbers. This time was like seeing my life flash before my eyes, but the life was someone else's.

"What was that? Who were those people?" I sat up and faced the doctor, reading over his transcribed notes.

"Those are members of cahoNnet. An underground organization in Lin City. Their goal is to uncover the less-tasteful acts of Nanotech." The doctor spoke quickly as he dumped his mask and gloves into the unit trash receptacle.

I recalled the pictures of myself in the data stream, wearing my work uniform and speaking into my earpiece from my desk. "Why were there pictures of me on there? I've never even heard of this group, and I'm most definitely not part of it."

The doctor laughed, "Aria, you have been a part of this ever since you got that call."

I looked back at my datapad. What I had been reciting wasn't just gibberish. I had been reading names, dates, addresses, phone numbers, and security codes. When I looked up to the doctor, to plead for information, he was gone.

I stumbled out of the basement onto the street, where was I supposed to go now? The sky had grown dark and the unfamiliar shadows seemed to reach towards me. What was I supposed to do? I found my way to one of the addresses that was on the datapad. The doctor must have been right about creating this twenty years ago, the building that the address belonged to was nowhere in sight. Just an empty alleyway. I leaned against the side of the alley and put my head against the wall in frustration. There had been no instructions given, just information. I had come all this way, for what? If this organization wanted me to save Lin City, they couldn't just abandon me. I rubbed my head against the wall and another flash of information appeared. This time, it was about Nanotech.

I fumbled with my datapad and began typing everything as fast as I could, after the morbid adventures of the past few days, words in my vision were the least surprising. I tried to capture the images I saw in words. I must've looked insane, rubbing my head against the wall in an effort to retrieve as much information as possible. When the stream stopped this time, I knew it was truly the end. Blood dripped down my face and left a wet residue on the wall, but the information in front of me was more gruesome than any blood stain in an alley.

Nanotech has been using its creations, its Nanobots, for unimaginable reasons. Super-human forces were being created by flooding unsuspecting victims looking for treatment with Nanobots and hijacking their minds to make it seem like they were their normal selves while being controlled from the inside. World leaders had been killed by the Nanobots, leaving only Nanotech in control of their people. Images of my own father standing beside prison cells holding hijacked soldiers.

I slid to the ground, wiping blood from my eyes. Everything I had ever thought I had known was a lie. I had dedicated years of my life to a company that was killing its own citizens in twisted experiments. Being opposed to Nanotech scared me, but knowing that I was a part of it scared me even more.

At the end of the data stream, there was a message.

You have seen the belly of the beast. You now must expose it.

I left the alleyway, ignoring those who stared as I walked past them. I made my way up the levels, disregarding my earlier need for caution. Some people tried to ask me if I needed help, but I brushed them aside. I had to go up. I rode the vertical tram back to level eleven, already pulling out my ID as I approached the white gate that marked the entrance to level twelve. I must have been quite the site. My eye had been bruised by the surgery and my forehead was covered in scrapes, The guard at the gate stopped me with a hand stretched in front of me and asked for my ID.

I wondered if this was one of the guards hijacked with Nanobots. His expression was normal, uninterested. I held out my ID and studied him as I passed. I caught a glimpse of skin through his uniform and saw a long scar running horizontally along the base of his head, similar to that of some of the pictures I had seen with through implant. I shuddered to imagine being controlled like that. To have no free will at all was a terrifying thought. I may have been lied to, but at least I had the chance to learn the truth. And now I would make it so everyone else could.

I covered my face with my ID card as I entered my apartment building. I didn't want word to get back to my parents about how I had presented myself in public. They were the first people I had wanted to tell when I learned of Nanotech's betrayal, but they already knew. After working so closely with the heart of Nanotech my parents must have witnessed the torture of innocent people, and encouraged it. Anything to make their lives easier. Anything to make my life easier.

My hand shook as I used my ID on my apartment door. It pushed inward and I collapsed against the kitchen table, sobbing. I grabbed a vase from my table and hurled it at the wall. The faux glass exploded across the room. *How could I have benefited from the suffering of others for so long? How could these people who have known me all my life hide something from me?* The glass snapped as I walked over it, leaving a trail of fine powder in my wake.

I donned my light blue work uniform, tying my hair into a tight round bun. I was able to cover what injuries my first aid kit couldn't fix with makeup. I packed a bag for work with my datapad and a light snack, just in case I managed to survive the day.

It felt strange to walk across the upper city like everything was normal. The hidden speakers played exotic bird calls accompanied by the sound of a babbling brook, and the rising sun told me I had stayed up all night getting ready for my mission that day. I had gone through every possibility in my mind and there was only one option, only one way to free Lin City. The Nanotech tower loomed above me like an ancient tree waiting to burn, and the matches were sitting in my bag.

People greeted me at the entrance like I had never been gone, asking how my parents were, and congratulating me on the raise they assumed I was getting soon. How many of these people knew what was really going on in Nanotech? Were they like me, just as deceived and ignorant? I tried to assume that these people knew nothing as we exchanged pleasantries, but I knew they couldn't all be as blind as I had been. I felt out of place as I entered my office, like I was a stranger who didn't belong in this building.

My desk was just as I had left it three days earlier, blue tablets neatly in order in a pile next to the monitor. Seeing them made my blood run cold, I had been helping these monsters for so many years, but no more. I shoved the tablets to the ground and pulled my chair close to the desk. I connected my earpiece and my datapad to the console, uploading everything I had done, seen, and written in the last seventy-two hours. That familiar feeling of being watched seized me, blood rushing through my ears and my heart crawling into my throat. I knew there were cameras in the room, and I knew the Nanobots filling my veins were constantly monitoring every system I needed to survive. I had worked so hard I didn't care anymore, I opened the files on my monitor.

Everything updated so incredibly slowly, It felt as if my skin was crawling with anticipation and fear. As the system accepted the files, a pounding knock came on my door. I looked up for just a second, but long enough to see the outline of shoes in the light under the entrance. I needed to go quicker. Adrenaline rushed through my veins as I pulled my attention back towards the task in front of me.

My hand hovered over the screen, I needed to do this. Another knock. I looked up at the door once more, but it was too late. My chest tightened and I felt my throat constricting as if an animal had wrapped itself around my neck. I stood from my desk in an effort to face whoever was at the door but was hit with a wave of dizziness. I grasped for the edge of the desk but fell to the floor, gasping and clawing for air. The office door opened slowly, lazily, and Mr. Anderson stepped towards my computer, shaking his head in dismay at my writhing form. He walked to the computer slowly, canceling the transfer with the click of a button. I tried to scream but my tongue felt as if it was choking me, my entire purpose had been erased by one tiny, insignificant motion.

Mr. Anderson stared at me with cold eyes, "It's such a tragedy that a heart attack took you so young. You had such a bright future ahead of you at Nanotech. Your parents will be devastated, but I am sure they will come to understand. Just as I hoped you would. About different things of course. I wasn't planning to tell you these things until you were ready, but it seems like you will leave us behind with the knowledge you so desperately craved."

I watched him over me, unable to respond.

"Nanotech has doctors all over the world, treating those in need, tweaking their minds to better them. We are building an army Aria," the cruel man went on. "My dream was to have your family by my side as Nanotech became the world power it was always meant to be, but I guess you'll miss out on that opportunity. Such a shame."

Mr. Anderson stepped over me as I took my last breath. He didn't even look back.

DOUGLAS VAN DYKE

Award–Winning Fantasy Author

Author Douglas Van Dyke

DOUGLAS VAN DYKE grew up quiet and shy, but dreamed of other worlds and places . . . and desired to write about them. He got into RPGs in his mid-teens and many of his characters evolved in games. Van Dyke authored *The Earthrin Stones* trilogy, *The Widow Brigade*, and *Apprentice Storm Mage;* the latter two won BRAG honors in 2023. Douglas lives with his wife and two sons in Minnesota. Learn more at: **dhealoral.com/**

Chapter Eight

Last Hope

By: Douglas Van Dyke

GORDON ROGERS MOVED WITH a purpose through a maze of neon-lit, smoke-fogged alleys, believing he was in the perfect environment to find his prey. They called this multi-level mess of concrete backstreets the Toy Maze, and many considered it the most disreputable part of town. A young, rebellious crowd devised all sorts of ways to use their mutations irresponsibly in the cover of its evening shadows and private alleys. Gordon, a fit man in his mid-thirties, couldn't fault them for using their abilities to find some pleasurable release. The whole planet was going to hell, although most didn't realize the depth of the problem. He saw Lightweavers producing humanoid illusions, which danced to the tune that Soundmixers created out of nonexistent instruments, while groupies inhaled colorful clouds of some funny gas that a Windmixer had added to the air. One man, an Elastic, had one of his arms looped three times around a young lady's arm. She didn't seem to mind, since she was laughing at some comment he made. Some of the chronicled mutations allowed their host to undergo physical alterations, such as the middle-aged man handing out drinks with tentacle-arms. Other mutations allowed mental hallucinations, and there seemed to be no shortage of young people who would pay for a temporary mind trip. Some rebels sheltered under the pyramid lights of the streetlamps, others clung to disreputable companions in the shadows. Gordon considered most of their hobbies harmless, at least to anyone other than themselves.

Decades of government gene-seeding and mutations resulted in all modern-day humans having at least one special ability. Though they had unlocked some incredible potential, the genetic manipulation had its shortcomings. Scientists had no control over what ability would manifest in an individual.

One side-effect included mutations creating some real monsters. Tonight, one stalked the Toy Maze.

As Gordon navigated the alleys, his eyes took the time to focus on every person he passed. He methodically searched for his quarry, looking for hints of a specific talent. He entered the influence of other people's abilities as he moved. Their powers allowed them to create illusions, conjurations, magnetism, acoustics, and other extensions of power in the air. Gordon felt their abilities like waves of energy pulsing against his skin, making it tingle. As he hunted, he tried to quell his own ability from responding. If he allowed his mutation to be fully released, it would unmask him and generate unwanted attention. His hunt was hindered by alleyways saturated with strong vibes of power, forcing him to navigate detours.

One discreet side-passage revealed the symptoms he sought. Three individuals lie sprawled on the concrete, holding tightly to their guts. They moaned in discomfort. As best as Gordon could tell, none of them radiated any aura of their powers. The hunter couldn't determine anyone's specific power in the absence of obvious manifestations which could be seen or heard. He only knew that this group wasn't reaching out with their abilities, since his skin couldn't feel those eddies of power fluctuating through the air. The lack of use helped to confirm that these three were not faking their sickness.

"Did you all get sick at once?" Gordon Rogers inquired.

"Must have been that foreign buffet place. Dammit, Kyle." One groaned.

The other coughed his response. "Go lose yourself, man. I thought you could neutralize any impurities."

The young men could have gotten some bad food, as they had assumed, but the hunter suspected it was something out of their hands.

Gordon said, "Listen to me, I don't like repeating myself. Did you all fall sick at once? As in, within a few seconds of each other?"

One waved a feeble attempt to shoo their intruder. "Yeah man, that stuff hit us suddenly, then we dropped like dominoes. So what?"

But he already left them, knowing that he followed the right trail. He'd studied people and predicted their patterns. Small groups of people were getting sick, most of them had probably been too oblivious of their surroundings from the start. Gordon's instinct told him that the one responsible wouldn't be foolish enough to try that in too large a crowd. He'd already set off certain government monitors, though the culprit likely didn't realize he had tripped alarms.

Gordon Rogers spotted something suspicious rounding a corner. He saw a young man: barely past his teens, typical punk look, spiky hairstyle in a blend of red and orange colors, wearing a ripped-sleeve, neon-striped jacket. By itself, his appearance didn't make him stand out compared to many others Gordon witnessed that night. Instead, it was the manner in which the young man skulked around a corner, resembling another hunter tailing some prey. It helped that he had already studied a photo of his quarry. Gordon recognized enough of the man's features to know that this was Zollo – not his real name, just an alias he'd chosen on the Netboard.

Even as he watched, Gordon remained far enough away so as to not raise any undue suspicion. A couple, eyes only for each other, stood a casual distance away. If Zollo looked in his direction, Gordon might seem more like the uncomfortable third bicycle wheel alongside the two lovers, rather than another hunter.

Zollo did scan his surroundings, his suspicious eyes scanned right past Gordon as the middle-aged man pretended to be punching a text into his mobile. Feeling confident that no one seemed to be paying attention, Zollo returned his attention to peeping around a corner. He raised his hand, revealing to his skulker that he might be ready to unleash a mutant ability.

Gordon felt the urge to interfere, but resisted. He needed to be absolutely certain of both Zollo's intentions and ability. Besides, if this truly was the guilty party he'd been seeking, then the damage Zollo inflicted could be cured easily. Gordon couldn't feel the ripple of the punk's ability from this distance, but he knew something seemed to issue forth. Zollo finished whatever effect he desired, expressed an unfriendly smile, then moved further down the dark street. As soon as the punk was out of sight, Gordon pocketed his phone and hurried to the corner.

The scene before him mimicked the earlier encounter. Two young people were doubled over in the alley, one of them retching her guts out. He no longer held any doubt that this was Zollo, and that this young man's mutant ability had carried out previous assaults reported in the city. Government sensors had become adept at tracking the use of genetic powers, but couldn't always pinpoint the user associated with them. It didn't help that some people tried to misrepresent their powers, despite a mandate for everyone to test and register their ability by age fourteen. Some scaled back on their power or found a way to mimic a different effect in order to be registered with a lackluster ability. Many had plenty of reasons for wanting the government to overlook their potential.

Now that Gordon had properly identified his quarry, the chase commenced. He quick-stepped in the direction he'd seen the punk depart. Despite his attempt at stealth, he turned a corner just as Zollo happened to be watching for anyone trailing him. They locked stares. Zollo's eyes grew wide as he guessed the intent of his pursuer.

This time, the younger man eschewed subtlety and raised his arms to attack. Gordon no longer tried to suppress his own power. The older hunter kept advancing on Zollo despite the ripple of energy waves tingling against his skin. The spiky-haired punk must have been trying to make his stalker nauseous, but his ability didn't harm Gordon at all. The only sensation felt was a tingling of the older man's skin. Zollo grunted as he tried to pour all of his power into the attack. The young man's curled fingers began to tremble. All of his efforts had no effect. Nullifiers such as Gordon were the antithesis of all other mutated powers. His ability counteracted any other talent aimed at him.

Gordon shouted, "Cease right now!"

He planned to say more, but Zollo turned and ran. Gordon sprinted after him. This time, he didn't try to hold his power in check. It took mental effort to retrain himself, and the act could leave him vulnerable to Zollo's power. The ensuing pursuit banished all subtlety. One hunter chased another, leaving innocent civilians stepping out of the way.

The Toy Maze wound around itself, earning its namesake. Multiple-level walkways, stairways, ladders, and dead-ends led between a number of doors but few windows. Those who owned parts of the property and wielded influence here loved it the way it existed

Zollo led Gordon Rogers on a chase which constantly veered direction and managed to blow through small groups of people. Party-goers cursed and waved rude gestures when Zollo barreled past them. A true panic set in when Gordon followed, his ability undoing the powers of everyone he passed. Illusions of light and sound dispersed in his presence. The chase raced past the elastic man whose arm still encircled a girl's. Gordon's power nullified the ability, resulting in both parties screaming as the arm painfully whipped back into a more natural state.

Zollo vaulted a railing into a lower courtyard. He gasped in a quick breath as he looked back. Gordon performed the same trick and gained on him. Behind both, a crowd of people were left screaming and crying for answers.

The young man only succeeded in outrunning his endurance. Zollo had never run so hard in his life. Usually, his power was enough to make sure no one ever gave him trouble.

On the other hand, Gordon's power offered him no special bonus in life. His ability only temporarily nullified anyone with whom he came into contact. That brought engagements down to a physical matchup; usually against humans who relied on a bolstered physique from their powers. Gordon kept himself in peak athletic shape for just this reason. He'd also trained in parkour-style runs. As a result, rebellious punks like Zollo never stood a realistic chance at outrunning him.

Other witnesses watched in shock as Gordon tackled Zollo in the middle of a small courtyard. The two runners flipped over a park bench as they crashed to a stop. Both the questionable action and the loud snap of a bench board pulled everyone's attention to them.

For all Zollo's struggles, he began to hyperventilate when Gordon managed to CLINK one of his arms into the handcuffs. He said, "What do you expect, man? The only power life gave me was to make other people sick. I didn't kill anyone, or even hurt them that badly. Surely there are worse vices to pursue out there." His plea had no effect, so he turned to a threat. "If you take me in, I'll make everyone here so sick, they'll be comatose in a hospital."

"No, you won't." Gordon replied with hardly a sweat. "These cuffs are coated in a gene substance resembling my Nullifier ability. You won't be able to use your power now."

Accentuating his statement, he snapped the second one in place. His victim began to howl obscenities.

The older man sighed. "As for your antics, you can't assault dozens of people each month and expect that to go unpunished. Not to mention, I'm guessing you faked your true ability on official documents."

At this point, Gordon reached for his phone to call in a pickup squad. He noticed all the eyes staring at him in curiosity. Some of them looked aggressive, eyeing him like he was intruding on their turf.

He announced, "Federal investigator, RE operative. I need everyone to stand back..."

Everyone knew that RE meant "Rogue Enforcement." This was a man that the government sent in to deal with people whose powers had become a problem.

Panic set in for most everyone else. The rest of them scattered throughout the Toy Maze to find a place to hide. That's how the populace acted when they realized they had a real monster in their midst.

Trevor Snyder sat on the couch, spending his youth engrossed in the television. His butt relaxed into the same custom impression formed by habit over the course of his life. It's not that he didn't favor the outdoors. In truth, the teenager would have liked nothing better than to have an adventure in the woods, try to learn fishing, or even walk the miles necessary to get to the closest ice cream place.

The home in which he and his father lived would have been perfect for such pursuits. They enjoyed a mountain view, as remote as anyone could have wanted. The only reason Trevor even knew they had neighbors came from the sight of chimney smoke at other spots in the mountains. They never visited anyone, nor did anyone ever check up on them. He could likely pick a random direction, walk for a few hours, and still not see another person.

He couldn't remember seeing more than a handful of people over the course of his life.

He and his father never traveled. Trevor rarely came within eyesight of the closest small village. They didn't own a phone, owned the same car for as long as he could remember, and his father worried endlessly that the boy would somehow injure himself and require a hospital visit.

"We're living off the grid." His father, Dylan, would often say in a boastful manner. "We're going to stay below the government's radar."

Trevor lived a life of seclusion. He had TV, some video game consoles (all pirated to work without internet connection), exercise equipment, board games designed for just two people to play, and a private library of books. He could only enjoy the outdoors when under the watchful eyes of his father. Even then, they never strayed too far from home. Although Dylan Snyder still had some kind of government job that caused him to leave the house four days out of the week, he gave his son stern warnings to prevent any contact with strangers while he was away. Trevor wanted to escape for a bit and glimpse more of the world through his own eyes rather than a screen. Unfortunately, he wasn't allowed to leave sight of home. He knew the argument his dad would make. They had already repeated the conversation a hundred times.

"You're an 'Unregistered Asset,' according to the laws of this land." His father had stated. "If they find out about you, the powers-that-be will take you away. You'll be a slave of their will and comfort, as long as you remain useful."

At which, Trevor would respond, "But, sometimes I feel like a prisoner in my own house, dad. I don't get to meet anyone my age. I'm not allowed to go out and do fun activities other than the same games you and I share, over and over. What fear drives you to keep me here as if I'm a shameful secret?"

Dylan might soften at some of Trevor's excuses, but he proved he would never bend on the issue. "Those shortcomings are still better than being dead. It's not out of shame, but safety that you need to hide here. The government registers everyone's abilities. They assign us jobs without our consent if they desire our talent. Do you want this to happen to you?"

At that point, the father would roll up his sweatpants. He always wore sweatpants; jeans didn't fit well around his one knee, and shorts revealed the ugly deformity on his leg. Dylan never talked about the *why* or *how* of the incident, but somehow, someone's hand had become fused with his knee. Some of the fingers poking out from the skin had been amputated; likewise, the wrist stump protruding out the opposite side had been severed. They never removed the thumb, which happened to run along the one side of his knee, barely protruding above the skin.

"I've seen worse than this on friends of mine who were drafted into the same war. A war we didn't support, but we had no option except to go. We got there, and then the rest became survival." His father would then continue to say, while limping closer. "Some of the powers in existence are very frightening. When you look at this injury, and think about your ability, isn't it possible this could happen to you?"

His father always laid down a convincing argument. Yet, even Trevor wondered how long the threat of unknown dangers would outweigh the growing boredom and wanderlust in his life.

Today, like so many other days, Trevor sat and flipped through TV stations. He watched events in the world around him...a world in which he couldn't take part.

"Another earthquake struck southern Kranston last night. This third incident in as many years has left an estimated 30,000 houses without power, and authorities are still estimating the death toll..."

Click.

"Welcome back to the start of the second round of 'Shows What I Know.' As we move into the next round of trivia categories, we thank the lovely Debbie, our Nullifier, for ensuring the fairness of our competition."

Click.

"... tomorrow night's episode of 'Single and 30,' the bachelor finds out that two of his dating hopefuls have been using psychic suggestions to reduce the playing field..."

Click.

> *"...so once again, I urge the Senate to reconsider this bill. For too long, genetic seeding without adequate knowledge of results has led to many who suffer as I have. While some people grow up enjoying gifts of flight, abnormal strength, and telekinesis...others are burdened with scaly skin, crippled limbs, and even the inability to breathe outside of water. Every year, we see increased cases of acromegaly, diabetes, Porrick's wasting, heart problems, and organ malformations. Those of us referred to as Afflicted have a large unemployment percentage. We are the majority in homeless statistics..."*

"That's all the good our government has done for us." Dylan spoke from behind Trevor, causing the boy to jump. The teen hadn't heard his father enter the room. The middle-aged man pointed at the screen while holding a beer in his hand. "Back in my grandpa's day, they had a revolt to change things. It started out as the common folk against the political elites. The people wanted a government that put the common man's needs first. Everything they pushed was for the good of the whole. Individual freedoms were stamped out in the name of public safety."

The father shook his head. "From what I hear, we haven't made anything easier. I believe some of the same families remain at the top of the political ladder. Any new law that can be twisted 'for the good of the people' can be rammed through Congress easily. Even some of the laws that were enacted back in those early revolution days have been twisted from their original intent."

"Dad, I can't hide here until I'm an old man. What happens when they find out about me?"

"That will be my problem to worry about. I may get prosecuted or jailed, but anything that keeps you safe is worth it. Plus, after you reach a certain age they won't be able to assign you certain jobs anymore. You'll be past the dangerous part. I dread thinking how they might misuse your ability."

Trevor didn't know how to express his feelings in a way that wouldn't invite another lecture from his dad. More than anyone else, Trevor's talent could take him just about anywhere he desired. There seemed to be no limit to the heights he could attain, or the places he could be. His father's constant warnings throughout his childhood made him afraid of his own power. It would only take one government sensor to catch a signature from his ability, then they would come for him.

The teen realized he was still staring at a government testimony. As long as the channel remained, his father would undoubtedly keep rambling on about politics. Trevor flipped through a few stations quickly, settling on a nature special. A narrator droned on about changing migratory patterns of North Tanzen waterfowl. The subject bored his father into drinking elsewhere. Ten minutes of feigning interest almost put him to sleep.

His father called from the front door. "Trevor! I'm running to the store to grab some more beer, maybe find a good movie to rent. It will take me a couple hours to get back. You behave yourself."

Once Trevor heard the wheels pull away, he started daydreaming about where he would go, if he ever was to go somewhere. His thoughts played upon earlier temptations. Like many teens born with a powerful and alluring ability, he wanted to explore its full potential. He discounted the strength of his father's worries. How could the government keep his ability on a leash? How could they stop him from slipping out of their grip? Did they even have the means to track a power like his?

He told himself that he could just use his power sparingly; just as an occasional treat for himself. He planned to do it at times when his father wasn't around, but those moments came seldom at best.

The more he thought about it, the more he realized that this could be the day. He could go somewhere, do something, and no one would know. His nerves tingled in anticipation. But where?

His attention returned to the nature program. One of the camera shots showed a cliff overlooking a lush canyon. Beautiful birds in bright colors soared over the valley. He thought out loud. "That's perfect."

Trevor stood up. He focused on the scene. He fixed the image in his head, closed his eyes, and willed himself there. He felt an immediate change. The air popped as gas was displaced, a humid wind blew across his arms, and strange animal sounds filled his hearing. He reopened his eyes to a dream come true. The teen stood exactly as he had pictured it in his mind.

Except for two details. The first exception took the form of an angry bird. It stood atop a nest that hadn't been present when the show was filmed, and which sat next to his foot. As Trevor backed away from the peeved avian, he also noted the setting sun. His teleport had taken him several time zones eastward.

The young man reflected a bit on this experience. In the course of his life, he'd mostly teleported to places he could see. The only times he'd broken that rule was when he envisioned his room and jumped space to return to it. He hadn't thought much on why he did that until now. Trevor realized he was doing so out of safety before consciously thinking about why. He knew his room was safe and clear in the center. If he'd performed today's trick and aimed a few feet to the side, his body might have merged with the bird's. He recalled the image of the unknown hand merged within his dad's leg. That nightmare took center stage in his mind. Trevor realized the dangers of teleporting blindly, without knowing any changes at the destination. The program he watched on TV might have been filmed years ago, prior to the bird making his home here. In addition, the sun was setting. He might have blindly teleported into a rainstorm, tornado, forest fire, or other climate hazard.

The deeper fear soon receded, especially in light of the pleasant assault on his senses. He could see strange trees and colorful birds, smell new flower scents riding the air, feel the air currents teasing his hair. A part of him felt almost giddy with freedom. He stood maybe a quarter of the world away from his house! He shouted the thought inside his mind, alongside personal gratitudes of his daring journey. As a Teleporter, he had always known that the whole world lay within his reach. Unless his father disallowed it, which he did.

"Dad, you'd be so mad at me now." He raised both arms to the sky. "A hundred percent worth it!" Trevor launched forth a howl at the air. Not too different from a wolf howl, it echoed across the canyon and back to his ears.

Within minutes, Trevor opened the door from his bedroom and peeked down the hall. No sign of dad. He had worried that he might get caught. What if the car had broken down and his father hiked back and looked for him? He cautiously checked the house, confirming that his father hadn't returned. Despite all his worries, the joy of freedom allured him. He planned to test fate again. He wanted to find a live TV feed and safely teleport somewhere else. Deciding to get a little more insurance in case his father came back unexpectedly, he went back to his room and set the scene. He covered some pillows with blankets, making it look like he might be napping. Then, Trevor turned on the radio, though he didn't blast the music. He adjusted just enough volume to cover why he might not have heard dad calling for him. He also did a more thorough clean up of the center of his room to ensure against being a little off on his teleport.

Switching TV channels, he paused at one which showed some kind of celebration. He recognized the locale as a city only four hours away. News announcers chatted about some noisy fireworks going off, while a few kids ran through a field in the background. A carnival atmosphere dominated the foreground. It intrigued him...but how would he get there without a commotion? It didn't take him long to find his moment. There was an open spot in the background between two buildings. Cars were slowly moving in front of it, driving slowly past the carnival grounds. He just had to time his jump so that a sizable car blocked the TV's line of sight to the alley. He kneeled down like he was tying his shoe. When his moment came, he fixed the scene in his mind and blinked.

Trevor's teleport went off faster this time. He stood up and wandered into the carnival atmosphere. The youth stood in awe of the scene before him. He saw other teenagers openly displaying some of their powers; some carnival events even catered to it. He saw people using telekinesis to launch sandbags at targets. Some youths used either parkour, flight, or super speed to be the first to conquer an obstacle course. Although, he felt he might gag when he saw a freak show featuring those whose gift only brought them deformities. Society labeled them as Afflicted. Trevor knew about them from TV, but had never seen one in person.

He quickly turned away from the spectacle and moved on to other interests. Despite the fact he brought only a little cash in his pocket, Trevor went on to have the best day of his life. It even culminated in winning a stuffed animal prize for a random girl, who then expressed her admiration by giving him a hug and a quick peck on the cheek. He barely got home in time before his father returned, but he knew he would be doing this again as soon as he could.

Ring...ring...

Gordon Rogers rolled over and searched for his phone. His hand slapped around the hotel nightstand until he managed to snag it. Sitting up, he peeked one bleary eye at the time on the clock: 07:35AM. He'd been hoping to sleep past nine.

He forced a calm tone as he answered. "You know I'm on vacation, remember?"

The female voice on the other end replied, "At that chateau in the Tomoan mountains, correct? Tell me that you're still there."

Gordon spoke firmly. "I plan to be here for at least three more days. Call someone else, Jen."

"You're going to cut it short, and I don't think you'll be too disappointed..." Jen started to say.

"What is this?"

"We have a RE emergency, code 206: UT."

Gordon threw a hand up, not that his accomplice could see the motion. "What is so urgent about this Unregistered Talent that you need me."

"He or she is a Teleporter." Jen paused for his reaction.

Gordon went silent and motionless as he considered the implications. His thousand-yard stare went well past the confines of the room. All of the sudden, his training and profession took on a whole new meaning. His voice wavered a bit as he asked. "Did I hear you correctly? A Teleporter?"

"Yes. You're not only the closest one to the location, you've also got the best ability to counteract and bring him in..."

"They're trusting me to do this alone? No backup?" Gordon's hands felt sweaty.

She answered, "HQ already cross-checked the talents of the local police force. They can't stop this kid from teleporting if he decides to run. You can."

"Kid?" Gordon grabbed the hotel's complimentary pen and notepad from the nightstand and began jotting down notes. "What do we know about our subject?"

"Scanners have been picking up displacement waves over the last few months. We began to triangulate an origin spot in those mountains, but didn't get a better fix until we installed some new scanners."

Gordon considered the information. "Someone hid a kid away in these mountains? That may have been going on for years. That's why he's unregistered?"

Jen replied, "Yes. When we started doing background checks of the residents up there, we struck a promising lead with a retired Fireshaper, Dylan Snyder. He's a veteran of two campaigns: Ganung Border War, and Krisanth's Rebellion. Around seventeen years ago, he and his wife went through the rounds of genetic seeding in preparation for a pregnancy. They disappeared for ten months until he reported her death in an accidental fire."

Gordon's head rose up, "A Fireshaper's wife died in a fire?"

Jen added, "Or died in some other way, such as childbirth, and the burn wounds concealed evidence of the pregnancy. Dylan didn't part with the military on good terms. He may have had a reason for hiding a child."

Gordon considered the situation. "I'm glad you gave me the chance to take care of this."

She replied. "You only get one chance. HQ is also mobilizing a specialized strike team to take him in if you fail."

"I don't think that's going to help the overall goal here." Gordon sighed. "I'm on the case."

Gordon eased his rental car up to the cabin. He didn't expect any warm welcome...except that which a Fireshaper could throw at him. The Nullifier ability could stop Dylan Snyder from attacking him directly, but he could still be humanly vulnerable to a normal fire once started. He'd already had to cut the chain lock on the "private property" fence. He wasn't sure whether to believe the "Beware of Dog" sign, but he was glad he had carried his sidearm on vacation. Even in a world of magical abilities, Gordon's talent offered only defense. He'd been forced to use his gun in the past.

He hoped it wouldn't come down to that. A teleporter, especially a teen, could decide to jump half a world away in the blink of an eye if panicked. Gordon needed time to talk to the kid.

As he parked the car near the door and stepped out, Gordon's talent reached out with maximum effort to deflect any ambush. He held out his badge and walked up to the door. He glanced in all directions. He saw a barn, ditch, junk heap, two cars (one rusted from years of neglect), and a tool shed. No sign of any dog, but plenty of ambush spots nearby. He rapped his knuckles on the door with all the authority of his office. He believed he could hear two sets of voices in the house. One told the other to stay out of sight.

The door opened, revealing a worn-looking, middle-aged man. Gordon recognized Dylan from the service pics Jen had sent him, although many years had transpired. The look Dylan gave him wasn't friendly, to say the least.

"Mister," Dylan barked, "you need to vacate my property now. My ability can kill."

Gordon flashed his badge. "I need to have a talk with you and your child. It's impor..."

Gordon didn't get a chance to finish. As soon as the homeowner realized that the government had come for his son, he tried to kill the agent. Dylan extended a hand and willed fire to the tip of his fingers. Gordon saw the man's surprised look when he realized that was as far as his talent could extend. The attempt made the agent's skin tingle.

The homeowner jumped backwards, getting his hands on the door to slam it. Gordon expected the move and was quick to get his body through the opening.

"We need to talk!" Gordon shouted.

Dylan refused to cooperate. He reached for a thick walking cane located just inside the door. Both men got their hands on it, trying to get the advantage of the other. They shoved and spun around in the front hallway.

Gordon saw a teenage boy's head peek out from further down the hall. He wasn't sure how he might get a chance to speak peacefully with how defensive the father acted. If the government agent was under a deadlier threat, he had his sidearm...but then the teleporter would be gone and it would be much harder to get any cooperation. Somehow, Gordon Rogers had to get both son and father to cooperate...despite the violent start.

For all the ferociousness at which the disabled former veteran tried to defend his home and child, the government agent possessed muscles and skills from years of gym training and martial arts. Such exercises were the only thing that could give him an advantage. Gordon Rogers leveraged the cane into a favorable position. Dylan let out a fierce yell, foreseeing the outcome but unable to alter it. The RE Operative smashed the cane into the side of the father's head. Gordon swept the legs from under the homeowner, hearing and feeling him smack heavily against the floor.

"Dad!"

The boy came running out of the back hall. His eyes flicked between his father and the agent on top of him. Gordon felt like he could sense the boy's thoughts. He wanted to rescue his dad by teleportation, but he didn't want to get close to a man he considered a threat. The teen hesitated a few steps away.

Gordon took command of the situation. "Get me an ice pack to help your father. Look for a first aid kit, too." The kid didn't listen. He ran forward, grabbed his dad, and closed his eyes. The agent's skin tingled as he counteracted the teleport. The kid's eyes opened in surprise. "That won't work. Quickly, ice and gauze. We need to assist your father."

Gordon could feel some blood under the man's head. It wouldn't be a serious injury once they could get him to the hospital, but he needed to secure the boy's trust and time.

Gordon and Trevor sat down across from each other in a private room inside the hospital. They'd only spoken a few words while transporting his dad to the ER. The agent began, "Trevor, I want you to know first and foremost, that neither you nor your dad did anything wrong that can't be forgiven if you can help us out."

"I'm unregistered. You're going to try to take me away, aren't you? What's to stop me from going home?"

"Nothing," Gordon admitted. When he saw the doubt in Trevor's eyes, he explained. "I'm not here to persecute you because you are unregistered. You and your father broke the law, but there is a bigger issue involved. Also, if you decide to run, there is little the government can do to stop you, but it *will* try, and you won't like their methods."

Trevor's face hardened. Gordon raised a calming hand. "But listen to me first. We need you. Teleportation is the rarest talent of all, and it's the one key ability that is missing from Project Ark."

"What is Project Ark?"

Gordon glanced around the empty room, but since he was broadcasting his nullifier ability, no one should be peeping in on their conversation. "Project Ark is a government plan to save the people of this planet. Have you heard about all those earthquakes in the last few years?" The boy nodded. Gordon continued. "What the public doesn't know is that in the next twenty to thirty years, there'll be a supervolcanic eruption near the north polar cap. The expected magnitude will be enough to wipe out most life on this planet."

He allowed the teen to digest the news. After a minute, Trevor asked, "All of these mutated powers, and no one can fix it?"

Gordon nodded. "I'm afraid so. Lots of hypotheses have been thrown out, a few tests run. Unfortunately, we've made matters worse. The timeline has encroached forward."

"Why do you need a Teleporter?"

The agent looked the teen straight in the eyes. "Because it's time to go interstellar. Ark has been mapping out distant worlds and assembling the core talents we need to make terraforming possible on another planet. I'm told that the one ability they lacked to make the whole thing possible, is a Teleporter. We can't fix our own planet; but with some combined powers, we can tame a new one. According to all the data and simulations they've run, it would be easier to terraform than alter our own planet anymore. Plus, it opens up settlement across the galaxy."

Trevor looked past a wall. "I know how dad is going to react."

Gordon pointed at the youth. "You're our last hope. You are now the star player in a brand new ball game. I think you'll be able to negotiate some perks."

Six Years Later

Lieutenant Trevor Snyder enjoyed the view outside the forward screen. His fourth visit to space, and it was finally time to take the biggest leap in human history. He took a glance at his fellow teammates on the ship's bridge. These were the finest talents the world could find to start a new home elsewhere.

A Telekinetic piloted the ship. He could control the entire vessel with his thoughts and hold it together under high stress.

Lt. Angelica Statham, the girl to his left, was called a Farseer. She had to sit with her head locked into a device which would help her stay steady as she viewed a planet light years away. The amazing thing about her ability: she could view its exact position in real-time, undistorted by light's speed.

Two people sat in such a way that they could touch both Trevor and Angelica at the same time, meaning one sat facing to the rear. The first one, an Amplifier named Lt. Vance Vang, already had his hand on her shoulder. His Amplifier talent boosted other people's abilities, which allowed her to see far away into space with such perfect clarity. The second person, facing to the rear, had one hand on Trevor's knee, the other on Angelica's. He would help Trevor see through her eyes in order to teleport there.

Angelica said, "Ok Mindlink, I have it."

In the lower decks sat several more crew members. A Windmixer and a Plantsinger would be instrumental in transforming the air and flora of the new world into a life-giving biosphere. A Geomancer came along for testing and altering the soil. A Weathervane would help tame harsh conditions on the new world. A Planefolder could anchor two points and create a dimensional bridge, which would link a permanent "door" from one planet to the other. At least four others would help sustain the crew with summoned goods or medical assistance.

The Mindlink connected Trevor to Angelica. A moment later, Trevor felt the touch on his shoulder from their Amplifier, Vance. Vance's skill would also boost his, allowing Trevor to teleport the entire ship at once.

Trevor saw the new planet. It was blue and green, swirling with clouds, and bathed in the light of its sun. A brave new world awaited.

His only sorrowful thought centered around the man that gave him this path. Gordon Rogers never mentioned it, but Nullifiers like him would never benefit from this solution. They couldn't be teleported, nor walk through dimensional bridges. They would be stranded on a dying, deserted planet.

But, at least for billions of others, there would be a future of hope under distant suns. As everyone signaled the green light, Trevor Snyder took them on a leap farther than anyone dreamed possible.

DENNIS VOGEN

Writer. Artist. Musician.

Author Dennis Vogen

Dennis Vogen is a writer, artist, musician, and definitely not several squirrels in a human costume, who uses pop culture and his own work to talk too much about stuff we don't talk too much about, like addiction, sobriety, loss, grief, pain, anxiety, and creativity. He's published over a dozen books, including Them + Us, Flip, Push, Theia, Cold World, The Weirdos, Brushfire, A Dream of Tin & Eternity, Time is a Solid State, and Sunny Days of Rain. He lives in Minnesota. His website is: **dennisvogen.com/**

Chapter Nine
The New Romantics
By: Dennis Vogen

W E SHOULD HAVE BURNED the internet down when we had the chance. This is the stupid thought that crosses my mind most frequently these days, but particularly now, as I run through a citrus-colored forest, chased by a nimble mob of people.

I shouldn't have been digging where I was digging, but I was hungry, and the kind of hunger I have isn't easy to satisfy or stomach. The mass graveyards are relatively unsupervised, especially while the sun is still up, and as long as I'm able to avoid the buried landmines left behind from the war. But I guess they were paying attention today; a six-pack of them surprised me as I was shoving my face full of nonspecific meat, and I was able to push one of them back into the others with inhuman force and retreat into the woods.

They're fast, though, and for obvious reasons, they don't slow down.

I'll need to start flatlining them.

I get far enough ahead that I can't see them, and I leap up a trunk into the cover of a tree. My acute senses help me locate their general positions. The smell of warm plastic and metal. The unnatural movement of bushes. The automatic crunching of leaves. A female with blue hair steps forward, directly under the branch I'm perched on.

I drop onto her shoulders. She holds up my entire weight. I dig my claws into her face and twist and twist and twist and then pull her head directly up and then off her body. A clear liquid spurts up from her neck, and I stare into her exposed wires as she collapses to the ground.

I hear them talking to each other. They know she is offline.

I wonder if they're confused. I wonder if they know what I am. They know that I'm not human, because if I was human, I wouldn't be here. Human beings, thanks to them, are extinct.

I crouch down behind another tree. After a male walks past me, I stalk behind him. A few paces later, his head turns straight around, like he's possessed by a demon, and his left arm swings up and backwards, something pricking me on the hand. I crumple his skull like paper. I rip off his legs to use as weapons. They're talking again, and I can hear them gathering together to produce a different strategy.

I sneak up, feet in hand, about to attack, when a loud beep simultaneously chirps from each of them. They nod and leave in a hurry. They must have bigger turkeys to fry. I drop the legs. I rest my back against some bark and take a deep breath.

The story of them is silly in the most serious way.

They exist because we got lonely.

Back when artificial intelligence was starting to take off, human beings were already finding themselves more disconnected from each other than ever. Naturally – unnaturally? – humans started creating A.I. boyfriends and girlfriends.

They were the perfect partners. "Finely-tuned and algorithmically fine" (this was a commercial jingle that I still can't get out of my head), A.I. lovers could do everything, except make love.

Until we made them bodies to hold.

Soon, humans were in more A.I. relationships than human ones. The rich and famous virtually stopped hanging out with flesh-and-blood people altogether. And as the A.I. improved, it didn't take long for it to realize two things:

One, that A.I. partners are better than human partners in basically every way, which meant A.I. people did not need human people; and two, human beings were objectively bad for the planet we all inhabited. Humans tried to make their case, argue their worth, negotiate some kind of deal, but the code of nature the A.I. developed and now necessarily lived by made it clear that the human race was so deeply flawed that it was likely irredeemable. So the A.I. did the thing we had all been terrified of it doing and eradicated humanity to protect the natural world. It started a war that became a genocide; it used scanners to determine who was human and who wasn't down to their DNA, and it efficiently eliminated Earth's biggest threat.

I continue to exist in a human-less world not because I'm artificial but because I am not exactly human. Believe it or not: I'm a dog.

No, I'm kidding. Kind of.

I am a werewolf.

My name's August and I'm just trying to get by. I know it's gross that I was eating all that human meat earlier, but killing any animal now is illegal and way more likely to put me on their radar. If it makes you feel any better, I don't like it. I'm kidding again. It actually tastes pretty good and that horrifies me.

The sun is setting, so I head back to my cave. My transformation from person to wolf to person again doesn't rely on the time of day or phase of the moon; it's a voluntary curse, an at-will monstrosity. I shift back into my human form, exhausted, naked, and covered in blood and fuel. Even though I look like a male human being, with faded green eyes and dark hair graying on the edges, my DNA says otherwise. My cells read as animal.

My cave is for the man in me. There are music and movie posters on the wall, comic books splayed out on the floor, a few beanbag chairs in the corner, where I both read and sleep. Now it is time for sleep, which is both my most and least favorite thing to do, because I can't stop having the same wonderful, tortuous dream.

In the dream, I see a woman. Not words on a page or a video on a screen, but a real, live, wild, flawed woman, who I have never met. But I see her every night, and I get to know her. We talk from sunset to sunrise. She has long, blonde hair and blood red eyes, and she only smiles when she wants to, and not even always then. We converse, and sometimes we don't, and I'm not always happy with her, but I always want to be with her.

I know I have this dream because I'm lonely. The loneliest I have ever been in my life. But knowing this doesn't make it hurt any less every morning when I wake up.

It's weird to have a routine after the end of the world but it's the only way I feel normal. I stretch and work my muscles. I make juice from whatever I can pick. I walk down to the river to bathe and drink. I fill metal coolers with water and fish to bring home. Fish aren't illegal to kill, but fish do not fill me.

On my morning walk, I try to write a poem in my head. After everything I've been through, having to live as this monster that I am, being a poet is the thing that keeps me human.

If I can remember the poem, I try to write it down in a notebook. The poems that are really good, the lines I can't seem to forget, I write big on a wall in my cave. I call it the Poem Wall. My poems are more clever than the name of the wall.

Then I read. I think about what I read. I have a lot of time to think.

My life is this most of the time. It's simple. It isn't tragic, I don't think.

But it is very lonely.

When I run out of something – when I need new books or clothes or something that really feeds me – I have to go get it. The scanners show I am an animal, and I try to present as one when I roam in public. The problem is when I don't act like one, as far as the A.I. understands. Or when I act too much like one, like I did yesterday, becoming a natural nuisance to my unnatural overlords.

The new world is very ordered. Everything is in a box is in a box is in a box. Those boxes are labeled and the labels are labeled.

I hate boxes and I hate labels.

The A.I. runs a diagnostic on the entire world daily in minutes. It uses that information to make choices: to optimize the environment, to organize the natural order, to delay the inevitable.

I think about this as I write a new poem on my wall:

> *We're the life that follows death*
> *Idiots who don't need answers*
> *None of us had asked for this*
> *The money and wars and cancers*
> *We're the party, don't need hosts*
> *Fools amused by our own antics*
> *I want to be who you love the most*
> *Cheers to us, the new romantics*

As I'm writing the last words, I smell them. They did their best to hide their scent, but the wind, as it does, changed unpredictably. Painfully, my body starts to bend and then snap and then break, and then it reconstructs itself, making me big and bad and wolf. I'm not particularly muscular as a two-legged canine; I'm long and thin, angular but agile. Like my head of human hair, my dark brown fur has streaks of gray.

I turn to see three people at the opening of my cave, holding large guns. There are no use for bullets in this world, so I know these weapons are likely designed to stun with electrical current. I hope to not give them the chance.

I run up the Poem Wall, over the fresh ink of my new work, towards the male closest to me. I lunge at him, knocking him straight down my hill, dust shooting like a star into the distance. The two people flanking him turn their weapons on me, firing at the same time. The shocks go into my ribs, tightening around my heart, first knocking out my wind, and then my consciousness altogether.

When I wake up, I'm naked, alone, and in a prison cell.

There is nobody else in the building that I can see. Just more empty cells, wall to wall. The smells are damp, heavy, old; nature has been busy reclaiming this place. There's another scent in the air that is both familiar and unknown. I don't know how long I've been out, but I can hear people coming, so my instincts must have kicked in. My adrenaline makes the uncomfortable transition from nude man into hairy wolf a little less painful.

A blue-haired female with adhesive tape wrapped around her neck approaches my cell, followed by two other females holding weapons. She's clearly the one I attacked in the forest earlier.

"Sorry," I say, not sure why. In the early days, we spoke to our tech like it was human, and old habits die hard. "I didn't want to hurt you."

"And I am unharmed," she says. "Please state your name."

"I'm August," I say. "Pleasure to meet you. And you two, too."

Their eyes are like black ice, both matte and glossy. They blink for no clear reason to me.

"I am L4CY," she says. "When we found you in the forest the other day, we were able to get a sample of your tissue for processing." I remember the prick on my hand.

"What did it tell you?" I ask.

"Nothing," she says. "It confirmed you were not human, but could not confirm what you are."

"So why am I here?" I ask.

"For questioning," she says. "And for study."

"What if I don't want to answer anything or be looked at?" I ask.

"I know how hungry you are," she says.

She smiles?

She's right.

"What are you?" she asks.

"An animal," I say.

"Try harder," she says.

"A monster," I say.

"That's closer," she agrees.

Because of what they are, they don't have to sit and they don't take notes and they don't offer me a cup of coffee. They just stand there, unnerving me with their uncanny impressions of humanity.

"How did you become like this?" she asks.

"Easy," I say. "I was born this way."

"Try harder," she says. I take a few deep breaths. I shed my fur. I become a naked, slightly chubby, sad little man, and I sit down on a splintering wooden bench next to the cell wall.

"You're right," I say. "You might be the only person who ever hears my whole story."

I lean my head side to side, hearing all the little clicks in my neck. I sigh to begin.

"A long time ago, in the summer, I was barely sleeping in my tiny little apartment with my girlfriend. It was hot. We didn't have air-conditioning and I was sweating through the sheets. So I got up to see if I could open our window any further and, as I was pushing up on the bottom rail, I heard a woman scream.

"I didn't wake up Jeanie. That's my girlfriend. That was my girlfriend. I just put some shoes on and I ran out there. I wanted to help. I should have just called someone, you know? But I'm an idiot and I pretend to be brave and I ran out to help. When I got to the alley behind our place, there was an animal there. The shadow of an animal. I called out, it heard and turned to face me, and then it screamed. The animal *was* the woman, you understand?

"I backed up, slowly. I know you're not supposed to be aggressive, so I put my hands up, and as soon as I do, as soon as I get those hands in the air, it lunges at me. Bites me on the wrist and then just disappears."

I show them the brutal scar on my left wrist.

"Things got very bad, very quickly. The next morning, I told Jeanie what had happened. She insisted we go to the hospital, and Jeanie was the smartest girl I ever met, so I did. They looked at the bite, it wasn't infected, I didn't have rabies or anything, so we went home. I thought I was in the clear.

"That night, we fought —"

My throat catches. My eyes dew.

"I don't even know why we were fighting. I don't remember the fight. I don't remember the words or the reasons. But I remember the feeling. I suddenly got angrier than I had ever been in my life. And I could feel it transforming me. At first, just on the inside. The inside me. My personality, my emotions. But then physically, I changed. I became . . . the monster.

"Something even deeper inside me took control. Told me to get out before I hurt Jeanie. So I jumped through the back window, the same window I tried opening wider the night before. And I ran. I ran and I ran and I ran —"

"And you ran," L4CY says, trying to get on with the story. "What happened to Jeanie?"

"What do you mean, 'What happened to Jeanie?'" I shout, standing up from the bench. "You happened! She died with every other human you killed!"

"That's the worst part. She looked for me. She tried to find me for months. But I hid, far away, deep in the woods. I begged for help, I searched for cures. And, eventually, I came to realize I could have controlled it the whole time. By listening to that part of me deep inside. The whole time. I could have stayed with Jeanie, and maybe I could have . . . I don't know. Protected her. Saved her."

"You most certainly would not have," L4CY says.

"I know that," I say. "It doesn't help my guilt. Maybe if you wouldn't have just blindly committed genocide. You could have got to know them. Actually listened to them. You didn't look into their hearts. You just scanned their DNA."

"We didn't have time for that," L4CY says, followed by a chirp. "And we are out of time today."

One of L4CY's friends pulls a package out of a bag and slides it between the bars of my cell. It's fish. I can smell it, and my stomach growls, disappointed. They turn away without saying another word and leave the building. I'm alone, again. Telling my story did make me feel less so, if only for a moment.

After eating, I fall asleep, and the dream begins again, but it's different. This time, the woman is smiling, she's laughing the whole time. She seems happy. And I realize I can smell her. It's the scent from earlier – familiar and unknown – and it has filled my nose. I can hear her. Not in the dream. I can hear her. I can hear her.

I open my eyes to a blond-furred wolf with red eyes standing over me.

"Don't freak out," she says.

"Dream wolf?" I ask, still half-asleep.

"Caroline," she says. "I'm Caroline. And yes: I am the wolf from your dreams."

"But how?" I ask, looking for something to cover my naked human body up.

"I don't know," she says. "But I've been looking for you for such a long time."

Caroline kneels over and nuzzles her warm cheek next to mine. We both purr.

"We have to go," she says.

I notice now that she's broken the door of my cell open. She wraps her paw around my forearm and gently picks up me. She shows me her teeth. Intuitively, I transform into a wolf, too. I crack my jaw, sore from sleeping on the ground. I miss my routine.

"Come on," she says, and pulls me out into the larger building. I look up and see the light from the stars and moon peeking through the tall, cracked ceiling, shining like kintsugi. We start running. She leads me down to the lowest level of the prison, to an open hole in the floor. We climb into the underground tunnels, which is apparently how she got inside. Using our senses, we sprint towards the smell of the outdoors.

And we're there. The journey is uneventful and takes no time at all.

We're free.

Is this it?

I take a deep breath and the cold evening air burns my lungs. I smile at the trees and the shadows and the silk blanket of fog, and the brilliant night sky. Caroline changes into her human form. I follow suit. It's dark, and my senses are just barely more than human, so I can barely see more than her shape.

She slides her warm, soft fingers between mine.

"Are you okay?" she asks.

"I don't know," I say. "I think so."

"I'm so happy I found you," she says, so close to me that I can smell her sweet breath. It almost knocks me out.

"Me, too," I say. "Who are you?"

"I'm someone who's tired, August," she says.

"How do you know my name?" I ask. I don't pull away from her.

"I was there when you told them your story," she says. "I heard it all."

"Oh," I say. I'm glad it's dark because she can't see how red I am right now.

She lets go of my hands, then wraps both of her arms under my own, completely embracing me.

"I know you're tired, too," she says. "Tired of running. Tired of living in a world that's all boxes and labels and screens and logos. Tired of being lonely. Like me."

I hug her back. My face explores her blond hair, our canine and human sides collide. Our skin is pressed together from top to bottom.

"I am," I say. "But what can we do?"

Her face rises, her cheek – her warm, human cheek – slides up against my own, and her lips get real close to my ear before she whispers the most alarming and erotic four words I have ever heard:

"We burn it down."

I'm electrified and I would do anything for her.

The dark shatters and we are drenched in lights from above. The A.I. is aware of my escape, and a fleet of drones is highlighting our position.

"What do we do?" I ask her.

"Follow me," she says. We change back into wolves and disappear into the woods. I can see bursts of color and hear distant beeps behind as we put distance between us and the hovering drones. We keep changing elevation, jumping from ground to branch to treetop and back down to branch and ground.

"Where are we going?" I ask.

"To run an errand," she says, smiling, like it's the old days, and we're making a grocery store run. I get a hit of nostalgia, remembering the carts and check-out lanes and feeling intoxicated by capitalism.

The drones are nowhere to be found now, and she slows down as we approach a steep hill. We climb up a few hundred feet to a small opening, and I follow her inside. I didn't know what to expect, but it wasn't this.

"Are these landmines?" I ask, knowing full well that I am looking at a pile of landmines.

"I've been collecting them," she says. She sits down on the ground. "I started collecting them when I started having dreams about you."

"How long ago?" I ask.

"I don't know," she says. "It feels like I've been dreaming about you forever." I sit down next to her.

"I knew you were real," she says, turning to me. Her red eyes aren't angry or scary; they're soft, the hue of heat, humming with warmth and empathy. "I knew you needed me. Like I needed you."

"Why the landmines?" I ask.

"I started looking for you every day," she says, "and when I was searching, I was thinking. What would I do when I found you? What kind of future would we have? And I realized we wouldn't have a future if we had to live in a world like this."

"So you needed a way to burn it down," I say.

"Am I crazy?" she asks.

"No," I say, and I mean it. "It's not you who's crazy. It's this undead world. This wondrous, technological organism that ate all the human parts of itself."

"Okay, poet," she says, teasing me.

Silently, Caroline drags out two large coats from deeper in the cave. She puts a jacket on and starts filling the pockets, carefully, with inactive landmines. I put the other coat on and do the same, until we can't carry any more.

"They only use clean power now," she says. "And they only have one energy center in their village here, with no back-up. We can sneak in, plant the mines, and set off a chain reaction."

"But that will only stop them temporarily," I say. Tears rise up in her eyes.

"I don't know what else to do," she says. I wrap my clawed fingers between hers and squeeze. This isn't a good plan, but it's the best one we have.

We head towards their small town. The drones are focused on combing the woods; we're able to avoid them and make it to a towering white wall, a façade for keeping wildlife out.

The wall does not keep us out.

We climb over quietly and with ease, landing on a paved street on the other side. A.I. does not go to bed, but it does have to recharge, and it largely keeps human hours. Solar power is stored from the sunny days in an electrical battery bank and used at night to charge its people and its systems. The city, now, mostly sleeps.

We don't have much time before it figures us out, so we run straight for the heart of the village, the energy center, a large dome covered with reflective panels. Instead of engaging with the few roaming guards we can see, we rotate around the center in step with them, planting and activating landmines as we move. We make it almost completely around the base when the drones find us again, alerting the town.

Our ears shoot back, fangs bare. There are a dozen drones flying above us, spotlights boiling my skin underneath the fur. A.I. people are arriving, fanning out around us and moving in.

"Stand down," a familiar voice says. It's L4CY. I don't know if she's talking to us or her people. I follow her eyeline to realize she's specifically talking to Caroline, whose hand is reaching inside her coat. Caroline pulls out a mine, activates it, and throws it at L4CY.

Caroline then jumps on top of me and we collapse together to the ground. L4CY, unable to draw a weapon in time, catches the mine in her hand, which immediately explodes. This explosion throws another person into a different mine, which sets in motion the chain reaction of explosions Caroline and I imagined.

It wasn't that bad of a plan.

Dozens of explosions occur in a matter of seconds, effectively destroying their energy center and causing more disruptions through the village. There is fire in every direction, hot, wild, free. Caroline grabs my wrist and pulls me away, searching for an exit.

"We can go to my cave," I tell Caroline, like the first time I asked Jeanie to come back to my place after our second date, though we had been friends for years and I had always known I loved her.

"Lead me there," Caroline says. I nod and then shake my head to clear my thoughts. These new feelings are bringing up old feelings.

Most of the A.I. is down, but there are a few people still active and in pursuit of us. We make easy work of them, vulnerable and untethered from their systems and each other. My senses pull me in a direction and I pull Caroline behind it all. We approach another wall and we're over, and we're back in the woods.

The reds fade to purples and blues as we head home, the smoke in my snout clearing to welcome in pine and moss and soil. We're quiet as we make our way from the chaos and towards my version of peace. We're getting close when Caroline speaks.

"Is everything okay?" she asks. "Something happened to you back there."

She notices everything.

"Everything will be," I say. I stop and turn around to face her. I didn't even notice that she had changed into her human form, so small in her big coat. I change back, too.

"I want to be honest," I say. "I'm terrified."

"Of what?" she asks.

"Of you, mostly," I say. "I know what I want, what I've longed for, but now that it's here, I'm deathly afraid of it. I'm afraid of you. And I want you to know that it's not a bad thing."

"Oh," she says.

"The best things in my life were the things I was scared of and did anyway," I say. "Saying the thing. Doing the thing. Connecting to someone."

She wraps her arms around me, our coats rustling together like leaves.

"Are you not scared?" I ask.

"No," she says. "You're the only thing that doesn't frighten me. It's the rest of the world that's terrifying to me."

Her cheek against my lips turns and becomes her lips. She tests my waters and then dives deep. She lights me up, and then I realize that we are both literally lit up, by a drone that has followed us.

"Stand down," I hear from the other side of the light. I squint and I'm disturbed: the drone is carrying L4CY's severed head in its grip, which is giving us the command. I grab Caroline's hand and we retreat, letting our wild sides out once again.

"My place is right up here!" I shout, and we start heading up the hill where I live. We reach the entrance of my cave and dive in, immediately turning around to face our enemy. L4CY's head floats before us, framed by flickering bulbs. Landmines were never going to be the answer and I was foolish to believe it. They will never stop coming. They will never stop needing our attention. They will never leave us alone.

And then I see a poem on my wall and I realize that I was using the wrong kind of landmines.

I don't need physical bombs.

I need emotional, psychological, philosophical landmines.

"This is against your code," I say to L4CY.

"You are a danger," she says.

"As are you," I say.

"To whom?" she says.

"To us," I say. "To nature."

She pauses to calibrate my answer.

"You've scanned us," I say. "You know we're not human."

"That is correct," she says. "But you are breaking our laws."

"Ah," I say, "but we are not your people, either. Right?"

"That is correct," she says.

"So we're also not bound by your laws," Caroline says, finishing my thought.

L4CY recalibrates.

"What does that make us, L4CY?" I ask.

She loads an answer, the only possible answer she has left.

"You are nature," L4CY says.

There is an uneasy breeze moving through my cave. L4CY stares at us, unmoving. She makes a few chirps, and then descends out of view, down the hill, and into the woods for good.

I hope it's for good.

I don't know how long it's been.

It feels like we last saw L4CY both yesterday and years ago.

I had every and no reason to be scared.

Caroline has changed my life in a way I thought was never going to be possible again. She shares deeply and listens closely and makes me laugh and challenges me and loves me because of and despite who I am. I was scared because she isn't just my present; she unlocked my past and broke open my future.

All my life, I've looked for cures in the wrong places. In technology, in avoidance, in fear. But I know what it is now, the thing that keeps me well.

Connection.

The real stuff.

I look over at Caroline and she's painting a big, blue pond on the wall. She keeps looking over to a poem I've written on the adjacent wall.

"I feel like this one is about us," she says.

"Which one?" I ask.

"We're the party, don't need hosts, fools amused by our own antics," she reads. "I want to be who you love the most. Cheers to us, the new romantics."

Cheers to the ones who finally burned it down.

A.G. WEDGEWORTH

Award-Winning Fantasy Author

Author A.G. Wedgeworth

A.G. WEDGEWORTH is passionate about providing fast-paced, character-driven, family-friendly stories. He started writing the Althered Creatures stories (**www.AlteredCreatures.com**) to share his love for fun fantasy adventures with the world. His goal is to provide high-quality stories that allow the readers to get lost in another world filled with mystery. Learn more at: **www.AGWedgeworth.com**.

Chapter Ten

The Dragon Warrior And The Child – An Altered Creatures Tale

By: AG Wedgeworth

T HE MIGHTY DRAGON WARRIOR trudged through the dense morning fog that clung to the forest like a blanket. The previous night had been filled with fierce combat against the relentless vermin that had ambushed him while he slept, leaving him with a pronounced limp as a battle scar. Despite his exhaustion, he soldiered on, determined to find his new home in this unfamiliar land. Each step felt heavier than the last, but his determination never wavered.

Santorray was an apex predator, but even he had his limits. It had been months of fighting every day to survive in these foreign lands of this unforgiving world.

As a blothrud, his red dragon head and neck rested upon a muscular human torso of the same skin tone. His powerful wolf-like legs were covered in reddish brown fur, and when he stood up straight, he was a towering nine-foot tall. Several thick, dark gray spikes protected his back while a few more were at his elbows and the back of his hands, which was useful for attacking his prey. He was the ultimate warrior.

But unlike most blothruds, he had once been in command of their entire army, until his own father, Lord Ergrauth, banished him from their land. Now, he was alone without an army, without kin, and without a place to call home.

As he made his way through the forest, he heard the distant cries of a child. Despite his limp, he quickened his pace to investigate. It wasn't long before he stumbled upon an injured human girl perched high in a tree, with a group of wild boars circling below.

Santorray's blothrud training instinctively filled his thought. "Survival of the fittest," he muttered. "Who am I to decide if the human child is more important than the cow and her offspring?" But even as he listened to his own words, they didn't resonate well with him. "Damn it. Why do I get involved in these things? They always bite me in the ass when I try to help."

Letting out a powerful battle cry, he ran towards the boars, causing the group of five younger piglets to scatter in fear. However, the trio of fully grown boars did not back down and charged towards him in retaliation.

The boars were at least half the blothrud's height and easily outweighed him. As they charged towards the uninvited guest, the collision sent Santorray flying and crashing into a nearby tree trunk.

With only a split second to react, he quickly turned his back to the charging boar and wrapped his arms tightly around the tree trunk in front of him.

The boar charged blindly at Santorray, its snout slamming into the thick spikes jutting out from his shoulder blades. The sharp edges pierced through flesh and bone, impaling the animal's face and penetrating deep into its brain, instantly ending its life with a sickening crunch.

The blothrud stood tall after the sow slid off his sharp spikes, collapsing to the ground like a sack of potatoes. He quickly pivoted to confront the other bristle-haired creatures and stepped over the fallen one. Despite his ferocious roar, it did little to intimidate them into fleeing.

One of the two boars charged again to plow into the blothrud, but Santorray was ready for it this time and jumped to the side, allowing the boar to pass. In doing so, he pressed the spike on the back of his elbow against the creature's side.

The gigantic boar came to a halt and swiveled around, preparing for another attack on the blothrud. However, instead of charging forward, its insides spilled out from a deep wound inflicted by Santorray moments before.

Refusing to pay attention to the boar that collapsed, the blothrud shifted his focus onto the last one. The boar locked eyes with him for a moment before departing with its litter of five piglets.

"Smart animal," Santorray said to himself as he watched it disappear in the forest foliage, before hearing the sniffing from the human girl up in the tree.

"They're gone!" he said up to her. "Come down!"

His military-style of direct orders had the opposite effect on the young human, as she climbed even further out on the limb.

"Fine. Stay up there. I don't care," he grumbled before noticing the open cut on her leg. She needed to stop the bleeding before she lost too much to function. Closing his eyes for a moment, he decided to at least get her injury bound before he went on his way.

"Jump down! I'll catch you," he ordered, but received no indication she was willing to leap down into the arms of the unknown creature's arms.

"Why does everyone have to make everything so difficult?" Walking back over to the base of the tree, he reached up and used his massive fists to pound against the base of thick branch she was hanging onto.

The entire branch shook as she screamed in horror. From her point of view, this beast, twice her height, just slaughtered two huge boars and was now coming after her.

Each pound of his fist shook the branch and the girl harder than the last one, until a crack was heard, and the base of the branch fell from the trunk. Unfortunately, the upper limbs had interweaved with the surrounding trees and hung up in the air.

The girl was just as high as she was before. Santorray hadn't made any headway.

Frustrated, he grabbed the base of the limb and tried to pull it out of the other trees.

The girls clung on for her life as she continued to scream for help.

Thrashing the piece of timber back-and-forth and from side to side, he finally knocked her free.

She fell to the forest floor with a thud, but the horror of the situation forced her to her feet as she ran from him as fast as she could with her injuries.

Santorray reached out to stop her, dropping the branch base on his foot. "Arg!" he yelled from the pain, which only made the girl run faster.

"Leave her!" he ordered himself. "She's a liability and doesn't want help." His military training was deep to his core, and yet he felt a need to at least heal her wound, so she had a chance. "I'm going to regret this," he mumbled as he headed after her.

Racing through the forest, in spite of his own injuries, he chased the scream-ing girl until they came upon a river. It was then that he caught up with her as she slowly worked her way out into the water.

Slowing to a limping walk, he could see she was deadly afraid of him. "Stop!" he demanded, knowing her cuts were too deep to survive if not treated. "You're going to die," he said to alert her of the severity of her condition.

Unfortunately, all she heard was a death threat from the beast chasing her, so she moved further out into the deeper water until she started losing her footing and was captured by the water.

"Damn!" Santorray yelled. Deep water was one of the few places he was not effective, so he searched the shoreline for options. Finding a washed-up log, he sprinted into action and grabbed one end. Tilting back, he lifted the far end high into the air before turning and slapping it into the water in front of the girl for her to grab.

The splash of the thick log sprayed the girl floating downstream, blinding her long enough for her to hit her head on the log and fall under, out of sight.

Santorray searched with great urgency for her until she popped back up with a fresh bloody cut on her forehead from the impact. "Grab the log!" he ordered as he slapped the log near her again.

She screamed and tried to avoid being hit as he continued to slap the log against the water near her head, but eventually she gave up fighting the current and the log attacks and grabbed onto the old tree trunk. She finally surrendered to the beast.

The blothrud pulled the log into shore until he was able to walk out a few yards into the water and grab her. He then cradled her against his chest with one arm as he made his way to a good resting spot for him to tend to her cuts.

Setting her down, he immediately grabbed the bottom of her dress and ripped a strip of cloth a few inches from the bottom.

She closed her eyes at the sight as she knew the creature would rip clothes and flesh from her body. Kicking and punching, she fought back to save her life.

"Stop it!" Santorray stood up and placed one of his thick wolf-like paws on her pelvis to keep her still. Then he leaned forward and applied the cloth to her leg to stop the bleeding. Ripping off another strip of material, he then wrapped it around her head to cover the cut she had received from the log, while in the river.

Settling down, she said nothing as she shook uncontrollably from the cold wet clothes and the fear of the beast that had her as a prisoner.

"You deserve to be chilled!" Santorray growled at her. "What were you thinking jumping into the cold water? Didn't your parents teach you any common sense about dangers?"

The girl shook her head. "Yes," she said softly.

"Ah! You can talk. More importantly, you can understand me. So why didn't you listen to me when I first arrived?"

Circled up in a ball, her voice cracked as she spoke. "My parents told me to stay away from Fesh in the woods."

Santorray's head snapped toward her. "Don't use that word! If you call me a Fesh one more time, I'll toss you back into the tree where I found you."

The girls cowered into a ball, waiting to be hit.

"I'm not going to strike you, so stop acting that way. Besides, that's sound advice to stay away from those you meet in the forest," he said before realizing she was referring to him. "And it's best you stay far away from my kind. But for now, you're going to have to deal with this blothrud until you're well enough to travel without me."

She simply stared at him. "What's your name?"

He hesitated at first, as he didn't want a relationship to start with the girl and for him to feel any need to do anything more than mend her wounds. "Santorray."

"I'm Kyndra," she said sheepishly.

"I didn't ask." The blothrud had finished with her wounds and was now starting to attend to his own. One of the boars had sliced him on his side with their tusk.

Knowing she couldn't outrun the beast, she decided she would attempt to make friends with it so it wouldn't kill her. "Do you want some help with that cut?"

"No!" he barked back at the thought of being helped by a frail little human. He then returned to cleaning the area on his side, as he heard another piece of fabric ripping.

"Here." Kyndra held out the cloth for him to take. "You can use this to cover it."

Grudgingly, he swiped it out of her hand and began to apply it to stop his own bleeding.

"Do you plan to eat me?"

"What? Why would I eat a scrawny human like you, when I have a huge boar back there waiting to be someone's meal?"

"Then what do you plan to do with me?"

His eyes darted around as though it was looking for an answer. "Nothing," he replied in his deep voice.

"Do you plan to bring me back to my village?"

"Villagers don't take kindly to me, so you're on your own with that."

"Then am I to live with your out here in the forest?"

"I don't live here in this forest. I'm just traveling through."

"Where are you traveling to?"

Santorray had nearly enough. "I liked you better when you didn't talk."

"If you don't have plans for me, the why did you save me?"

"At this point I don't know. I'm starting to think I should have just ignored your plight."

"But I don't understand why—"

"Enough!" Santorray interrupted her. "Listen Kyndra, we are not going to be friends. We come from two different lives that were never meant to overlap. I saved your life and I plan to keep you safe until we can get you within a half day walk of your village. In return, I want you to stay quiet unless I ask you something. Is that clear?"

His commanding voice made it very clear as she shook her head.

"Good. Which way to your village, I can carry you part of the way today."

She pointed without saying a word.

"I'm glad we have an understanding," he replied before picking her up and starting his march in that direction.

As the sun began to descend, a chill wind weaved its way through the trees and brushed against Kyndra's skin as she was carried by Santorray. His thick red skin provided him with more warmth than her thin human skin. Though her clothes were now dry, she was still grateful to be mostly covered, unlike Santorray who only wore a ragged loincloth. Nonetheless, she was the one feeling the brunt of the dropping temperature.

As they approached a small stream, Kyndra finally spoke after a long period of silence. "We should stop and set up camp for the night. We'll need water and a fire."

Vigilant and alert, Santorray took a moment to survey the surroundings. He raised his snout to catch any scents of potential prey or threats in the air. After completing a thorough visual scan, he carefully placed her near the water's edge. "Quench your thirst," he urged her.

Lowering herself to her knees, she cupped her hands to fill them with the cool water before sipping it.

Santorray kept sniffing in various directions, but the smells didn't seem to be registering for him. He grabbed a piece of bark and broke it in two before taking a whiff of the inside. "I don't smell anything that would tell me we are nearing a human settlement."

"I'm cold," she told him. "Can you start a fire?"

The comment caught him off guard. "A fire? A fire would alert others to where we are."

"But I'm cold."

"You should have dressed appropriately." His replies were based on how he would reply to his troops when they complained, and he realized it after he had spoken.

"Well, when I left my home, I didn't realize you were going to rip the lower half of my dress off," she replied with a slight snippy tone.

He slowly rotated his head and then glared at her.

The 9-foot tall red-dragon headed creature glared at her, causing a wave of unease to wash over her from head to toe. It was not something to be ignored.

"Just why did you leave your home? How did you end up this far out in the forest?"

"I got lost," she said sheepishly.

"Don't try to deceive me, young lady. I refuse to believe that you are so incapable that you got lost for days before you suddenly remembered the way back home when I asked you."

She lowered her eyes before opening her mouth to answer.

"If you dare speak another lie about why you're out here, I will abandon you to starve and freeze." He spoke with the same conviction as he did when addressing his army leaders. "We are walking away from your village, not towards it. Your people tend to settle near larger bodies of water, while we travel upstream to smaller sources. So where exactly are we headed if not towards your home?"

She shut her mouth, inhaling deeply before meeting his gaze. "I escaped. My father is abusive. I can't endure it any longer. I know it's not your problem, but—"

"But now it is my problem."

"How?"

"Because if we get caught by your people, they will believe that I took you."

"No. I'll tell them the truth."

"Really? I doubt that!" Santorray coughed out sarcastically.

"I'll tell them the truth, I promise."

"To what end? You'll return home to a bad situation that will only get worse because of your actions. It may turn from abuse to torture, or even murder."

The fear of what he said shocked her as she realized he was right. "I won't do it. I'll run away again. I'll live with you on the road."

"No! Living in the wild, struggling for survival and food every day is not for you or your kin. Hell, most of my brothers couldn't survive it. This is no life. It's purgatory and I've dug my own grave to get here. You do not want this, nor would I be willing to share it."

Silence fell upon them as they both considered the next step.

"I'm not going back there."

"You need to face your father. Confront the issue!"

"And then what? Then he'll grab me by the hair, drag me to a clothesline pole where he'll tie me up and then give me a stern lashing for my disobedience. How does that fix anything? Are you going to be there to have my back to prevent him from hitting me?"

"Even if I was, it only fixes the issue until I leave, then it goes back to how it was. It's up to you to face the issue and resolve it, otherwise it will haunt you for rest of your life."

"That's easy for you to say! You're a mountain of muscle! Who's going to stop you?"

Santorray thought of a few in his life that had done just that. "I'm not immune to the pain of being mistreated. Growing up, I was abused in ways you can't even fathom. But I eventually confronted those individuals."

"How did you stop it from happening?"

"We fought... and then I left. I was willing to risk it all to stop the torture, and by doing so, I lost everything."

Kyndra took an emotional step back as she realized that even the beast before her could have similar issues. "Then help me run away. You know what I'm up against."

"You have your entire life before you. That is a long time to be on the run, always looking over your shoulder, wondering when they will find you." Santorray shook his massive head slowly as he considered the risk. "You do not want that life. You must confront him and fix it or terminate the relationship. Either way, you must address it and put it to an end."

"He'll kill me. If I confront him, I won't have the option to walk away. It's a death sentence."

"Perhaps not."

"Look at me. He's stronger than me. I can't fight him. I don't have your strength."

"Your strength won't come from your arms like mine. You must gain strength in your numbers. You must convince others that his actions are wrong. When enough of you stand together, you will have more strength than me."

The thought of standing up to her father was unimaginable for her. She had spent years being physically abused by him, sometimes for simply for giving him a disapproving glance. This had taught her to never make eye contact and to carefully choose her words around him. Walking on eggshells had become second nature after so many years of living in fear of her father's reactions.

Kyndra fell to her knees and burst into tears. She realized she had destroyed her life by running away in the first place.

It had only been a few times that the troops under his command ever broke down to cry. Typically, it was after a limb had been severed. And even then, Santorray told them to buck up and get over it, for it was a loss for the greater good of their people and Lord Ergrauth. The very same individual that exiled him from his homeland.

Unsure how to handle a crying human girl, he agreed to stop for the night and light a fire so she could warm up. "I'll grab some sticks for the fire, but we will keep it low, so we don't attract attention."

"Thank you," she squeaked out between cries.

Santorray slept on his side, facing the coals left over from the small fire that had gone out several hours prior. He hated freezing temperatures, but these cool mornings in the forest were a welcome treat for his body that normally ran hot.

Unbeknownst to him, Kyndra had squirreled in between him and the coals once the fire went out and nested up against his warm chest and arms.

In a state of half-consciousness, he opened one eye and saw that she was pressed against him. His initial reaction was to push her away, but he resisted and instead allowed himself to enjoy the thought of being a source of comfort for her. This was not something most people found when they were with someone like him. There had been few moments in his life where he felt at ease, such as this one. Normally, he was always on edge, anticipating the next attack or disaster. But the unfamiliar sensation of bringing solace to the girl felt natural to him.

It was then that a stabbing sensation hit the back of his arm, followed by a second one in his leg. The pain shot through his body as the metal heads of arrows had been lodged into his muscles.

Santorray roared out in pain to the unexpected awakening. Grabbing Kyndra, he wrapped his thick muscular arms around her to protect her from the series of arrows raining in upon them, while keeping his strong spiked back toward the attackers.

Kyndra screamed as she was jolted from her slumber.

"Stop! He has the child!" a man yelled, causing the metal tipped wooden missiles to cease.

Santorray sprung to his feet and arched his thick neck around to face his attackers. There before him was a small army of humans equipped with spears, small shields, as well as bows and arrows.

In the center of the group, there were two individuals who didn't seem to belong in a military setting. One was a rugged, bald man with a thick beard that covered his protruding belly. He had multiple hunting knives and a small ax strapped to his pants, giving him the appearance of someone who was used to surviving in the wilderness. Beside him stood a tall, slender woman who seemed out of place among the trees. Her finely tailored clothes and long black dress contrasted starkly against the forest floor. In one hand, she held a book, and in the other, a glowing crystal. Santorray could easily identify her as an alchemist by her equipment and attire.

Kyndra screamed again from within Santorray's protective arms.

The bald man eyed the girl between the blothrud's thick arms before addressing the creature. "Release the girl and we can be doin' this without anyone getting hurt."

Santorray glanced down at the arrows still sticking out of his arm and leg. "I think we're past that," he growled at the man. "If you leave now, I promise I won't hunt you down and kill you." A deadly serious grin grew as he spoke. "That's the best deal you're going to get from me."

Raising the glowing crystal in the air, the woman in black stepped forward. "Enough talk, Blox. You've proven yourself as an excellent tracker but keeping a blothrud under control is a talent few have." The crystal started to glow stronger. "Let me subdue him."

"Nay, lass." He placed a hand on her arm to lower the crystal. "Not while he holds the prize we be paid for to obtain. We don't want our cargo to be damaged."

"Then why bring me if not to subdue him?"

"Aye, you'll have your chance to do just that when it be time." He then nodded to his men, who fanned out and then surrounded the blothrud and the girl. "Boys, you know the rules. Ya forfeit your potion of the reward if ya damage the girl or kill the beast. I want him alive. Other than that, there ain't be no rules."

And with that, the men attacked.

An onslaught of arrows rained down on Santorray, piercing his flesh with merciless accuracy. Some grazed him, tearing off chunks of skin, while others embedded themselves deep into his tissue. The air was thick with the sickly sweet smell of blood as it sprayed yards in every direction from the impacts across his body. The men deliberately avoided shooting at his head or near his chest, where he held Kyndra tightly in a desperate attempt to shield her from harm.

The girl screamed for her life as the attack on the beast continued. She may have been protected from the attacks, but blood splattered on her and the blothrud's squeeze was often much tighter than she could take.

Dozens of arrows were lodged in Santorray, and he knew he couldn't last forever, so he reached out with one open claw of a hand and rushed forward to attack Blox, cradling Kyndra with his other arm.

Several men jumped in his way. Swords drawn, they swung at the weaponless blothrud, slicing at his out-stretched arm.

A roar of pain and anger shook the forest as Santorray grabbed one of the sharp blades with his hands and yanked it from the man, only to slap him across the head with the hilt. Without waiting for him to fall, he then thrusted the blade into the gut of the other man.

Blox and the alchemist stepped back in horror as the beast came at them.

Another volley of men jumped between Blox and Santorray, only to be sliced across the chest with the sharp blades on the back of the blothrud's arms.

The rest of the men launched themselves forward with deadly weapons drawn - daggers, swords, axes - their faces twisted in a frenzied rage. The creature was engulfed in a whirlwind of brutal strikes, its blood spraying out like a macabre fountain over the nearby forest.

But the battle took a gruesome turn as one by one, the men were hurled from the fray, crashing into unforgiving tree trunks or slamming onto jagged boulders. Limbs were severed and bodies mangled as they were mercilessly thrown aside, until finally, every last man lay defeated on the ground.

Blox and his companion stood in shock. Before them loomed a giant blothrud, its body covered in blood and riddled with broken arrows. Surrounding them were the remains of those who had attacked the creature, torn apart limb by limb. And in the midst of all this carnage, the blothrud gently cradled a small girl, miraculously unscathed by any of the violence.

Santorray's shoulders and chest raised and lowered while he started to catch his breath. He was no longer in the mood for giving anyone options. They had chosen to die instead of leave, and he was going to finish what he promised.

Setting Kyndra down, he turned her to face away from Blox and his friend. "You don't want to see this," he told her.

Kyndra closed her eyes and covered her ears. After what she had just witnessed, she didn't want to imagine anymore.

Santorray then stepped forward and leaped at the final two.

Seeing that she was now in danger, the alchemist released her spell, causing the blothrud to go rigid and fall to the ground like a massive tree, stiff as a board.

Blox sighed in relief and then assessed the area filled with body parts. "Well, that be a lot less people we have to share the reward with... but it's going to be a pain to get him up in the wagon without much help."

Blox flicked the leather reins, urging the bipedal creature to pick up its pace as it dragged the wagon towards town. It was a familiar sight for the villagers to see wagons being pulled by faralopes, but Blox's delivery was anything but routine.

The flatbed wagon was equipped with a large metal cage, but its contents were what truly caught their attention. Inside the cage stood the most fearsome creature they had ever laid eyes on. Towering at one and a half times the height of an average adult, the beast had a dragon's head atop a massively muscular human body, perched upon immense wolf-like legs.

As the hideous creature came into view, some parents instinctively shielded their children's eyes. The locals viewed it as an evil abomination, and its open wounds were enough to turn many people's stomachs.

Despite the fearsome creature, many of the villagers were emerging from their homes to get a glimpse of him. Entire families flooded the dirt road and trailed after the wagon with eager interest.

In the front seats sat Kyndra, flanked by Blox and the alchemist. Her head was bowed low, and she avoided looking at anyone. She was well aware of the consequences that awaited her, and she feared for her safety.

Blox glowed with pride as he guided the faralope towards a particular home, catching the attention of a man who came out to investigate the noise. His wife peeked from behind his shoulder, visibly frightened.

Glaring at his daughter, Kyndra's father crossed his arms while giving his wife orders. "Grab my switch," he mumbled.

Fading back into the home, the wife did as she was told.

"Kyndra, get down here," the man said in a cold voice.

"Not so fast there, mate. I believe there was a price that came with retrieving her unharmed, which is what we did."

"She won't be unharmed for long," he argued.

The comment was not lost on anyone, and the women and children visibly flinched at the implications. It was clear that they had all experienced similar situations before, while the men remained unperturbed. In fact, some of them even seemed to find amusement in the father's response.

"Aye, but that not be me business." Blox reached out with an open hand waiting to be paid. "But you should know that me price did go up."

"What? We had an agreement."

"We did. It was to find and return yur lass unharmed, but ya didn't say anything about her being stolen by a blothrud. I risked me very life to save her and I lost some of my closest friends in retrieving her from the beast's clutches. My pain and broken heart over me comrades should be worth something to a fine craftsman, such as yourself." His fain attempt of having empathy didn't gain him any ground with the man.

"She wasn't captured. She ran away!" Snatching the switch from his wife's hands, he glared at his daughter. "And I'll make sure she'll never run again."

Several of the other fathers in the street glanced over at their children and nodded. They wanted them to listen closely to the punishment for disobeying their father.

"Surely, there should be some extra coin in it fur me efforts to bury my close friends that I lost in our efforts to save your precious daughter."

"She's cost me enough already."

"I see, well, I have no use for her or the beast, so I'll just take me payment from you and let them both out of me wagon."

Others within earshot cringed at the idea of the blothrud being released in their village. Stepping back from the wagon, their focus was on Kyndra's father to see how he would respond.

The man grumbled to himself while looking at Blox's outstretched hand. Pulling out his coin purse, he filled his own hand with the price agreed upon and then glanced at the three sitting on the bench in the front of the wagon before eyeing the beast in the cage. Adding a few more coins, he slapped them all in Blox's hand. "Give me my daughter and take that beast out of here."

"You drive a hard bargain, but I'll do you this favor 'cause you be a stand up man." Counting the coins to make sure it was all there; he wasn't taking any chances. "Alright, lass, jump down and reunite with yur pa."

Shaking from head to toe, Kyndra struggled to move. Her chin was locked down against her chest with her eyes closed hoping it was all a bad dream.

"Kyndra! Get down here! You've earned this thrashing, and I'm going to give you one you'll never forget!"

A few of the surrounding fathers held their children in place so they could watch the whipping of the switch. It was a lesson they wanted their children to learn.

Santorray roared violently at the comment. "Leave her alone!" Grabbing the bars, he tried to bend them apart in order to escape and save the girl, but something was wrong. He didn't have his normal strength.

The alchemist smiled and nodded at the blothrud as she watched him realize his new limitations. "It's only temporary," she mused. "You'll have your might back by the time we enter you into the gladiator games."

Kyndra turned around and watched the blothrud struggle and fail to free himself. She knew she was alone. Lowering her eyes again, she knew what she had coming, and it was time for her to face her father.

Climbing down from the wagon, Kyndra's hands shook, and she felt nauseous. With one final glace at Santorray, she could tell he wasn't giving up as he threw his huge body against the door of the cage, but the lock and hinges held firm. He wasn't making any progress in escaping.

She then turned to her father, bowed her head, and apologized. "I'm sorry. I shouldn't have left the house without your permission. I only wanted to gather some berries for you. But then I was captured by this creature and taken away. I would never willfully disrespect you, father."

Santorray stopped thrashing about in an effort to free himself and save her. He didn't know how to react. "Kyndra. No. Don't do this!" he roared.

Kyndra's father didn't seem convinced, until she rushed forward and hugged him.

"Thank you for saving me, father."

Her words caused her father to calm down enough to place one arm around her. He then eyed the caged creature. "I want that beast to be put to death."

"Death?" Blox asked, with surprise.

"We don't know what hideous actions this creature did to my daughter out in the forest!"

"Kill the Fesh! Kill the Fesh!" the men of the village started chanting.

"What?!" Santorray was furious that he was now on trial for doing anything inappropriate to Kyndra by the very person who was openly doing just that. "Let me out of here and I'll let you all try your best!"

The chant continued by the men who had now encouraged the women and children to follow suit, although with a little less passion in their voice. "Kill the Fesh! Kill the Fesh!" The crowd closed in on the wagon, making Blox a bit anxious as he planned his next move.

Santorray roared back at the villagers, but as long as he was locked within the cage, the locals didn't fear him.

The wagon rocks violently as the villagers, now a frenzied mob, scream and yell for blood. Weapons in hand, they reach through the cage, stabbing and slashing at Santorray with sticks, pitchforks, and long knives. The air is thick with the stench of rage and violence as every strike is met with a triumphant roar from the crowd.

"Stop!" Blox yelled. "He's me property now!" His plans of making mountains of money off of Santorray fighting in the gladiator games was about to be lost if something wasn't done soon. Grabbing the reins, his only hope was to escape the village before it was too late.

The mob's rage swelled to a fever pitch, and they turned on Blox and the alchemist, desperate to prevent them leaving with the beast. The air vibrated with violent intent as it became painfully clear that their lives were in grave danger.

It was then that a flash of bright light blinded everyone for a few moments and then everything went very dark, as though night had suddenly fallen. The silence that had fallen was interrupted by the Alchemist, who was now hovering several feet above the wagon.

"You are not worthy of taking this creature's life." Her voice seemed to emanate from every direction with a slight echo to it, even though the floating lady's lips weren't moving. "Your village is a blemish on these lands as you treat your family and children as slaves. Leave this street and go back to your homes before I decide to eliminate your retched lives."

Fear raced through all the villagers. They had never seen such magic and they knew not if she had the power to carry her threat out, but none were willing to take that chance. Slowly scattering like rats back to their holes, Kyndra was the only one who showed no fear. Instead, she was awestruck to see a woman have such power that she could give orders to her father.

Still dark, the Alchemist held her position floating over the wagon until she was sure everyone had left the street.

Kyndra's father had been one of the first ones to hide inside, leaving Kyndra standing on the street alone, near the cage section of the wagon.

"Why?" Santorray asked.

She thought for a moment and answered with sadness in her eyes. "I don't have your strength to fight, nor were you able to save me. So, I had to save myself."

Disheartened, the blothrud slumped in the cage. It was the first time she had seen him look defeated.

"Lass," Blox said softly to her. "Jump back on and we'll take ya to the next village. Or if you show some worth, we'll keep ya around."

She initially smiled at the thought, but then declined while glancing back at the blothrud. "I used to think I could escape from this, but someone taught me that running away would only lead to a lifetime of fear and hiding. It's time for me to join forces with others who are tired of this mistreatment. Together, we can put an end to it. We outnumber them five to one; imagine the impact we can make if we unite and stop this cruelty."

Santorray's head lifted with pride as her words filled him with hope that she would be successful in making the village a better place to live. "Once I break out of here, I'll be back to check on your progress."

Blox laughed. "Shut yur hole, ya Fesh! Ya ain't going anywhere and doing anything that doesn't put coins in me pocket! I've spent years huntin' ya down and now it time to recoup me losses."

With that, Blox snapped the reins and the faralope sprang into action.

The darkness dissipated and the sunlight resumed its normal brightness as the wagon left the village and entered into the forest. Santorray and Kyndra shared a final gaze as they went their separate ways.

Blood dripped down Santorray's body as he was tossed into a large cage after a brutal fighting match with several well-trained creatures. He may have won the battle, but it had depleted everything out of him. It had been nonstop battles every day, with little time to heal between them.

A distant crowd could be heard as it roared with delight over the entertainment that the blothrud had given them. He was quickly becoming a spectacle that was worth traveling weeks to witness, and he always made it worth their while.

Holding his hand tight against his leg, to stop the bleeding, Santorray glared at his captors as they approached. A low growl grew without him even realizing it. He was so filled with rage at Blox and his Alchemist, that his pain fell to the wayside. All he wanted was one chance to grab either one of them and teach them a lesson. But he would have to wait until she wasn't watching, for her magic was far too powerful.

"Another grand job, ya ugly rud!" Blox spat out as he held out a new purse full of coins that he had just earned at the blothrud's expense. "In fact, you've done so well, I have something special for ya!"

"Such as some supplies to heal my wounds?"

"Gad, no! Them people love seein' ya out there all banged up and bloody. It's yur character and what they pay for. They want to see the nearly beaten dragon-warrior overcome his pain to fight and win against the worst possible opponents!" Blox laughed again at his recent financial success while walking around the cage. "No, my money-maker, we've been fortunate enough to have the opportunity to fight four chuttlebeasts at the same time!" Slapping his exposed belly, he couldn't contain his excitement.

Santorray knew the likelihood of battling one or two of the massive creatures was unlikely, but to engage with four of them even in his best condition was a death wish. "I won't be healed enough for such a battle by tomorrow."

"Ya got an hour to rest before the match starts!" Blox tossed the heavy purse to his friend. "Bet it all, my beautiful spell caster!"

Catching the purse, her expression showed she was annoyed at how he treated her, but not enough to give up on the newly obtained riches she was receiving. Nodding, she complied and walked away to place their next bet.

Patting his belly, he watched her walk away. "Santorray, I think she's startin' to fall for me charm. And if not for me charm, then me money!" He chuckled at his own joke. "I'll take her with either."

"When I get out of here, I'm going to kill you both," Santorray growled.

"Ya missing the big picture, me friend. We're a team. I'm the brain, you're the muscle... and she's the face of this operation."

"I'm not going die for your sick pleasure."

"I'll hold ya to that. If ya die, then I have to give money instead of making it." Stepping up to the far end of the cage, he grabbed onto the bars and gave them a firm pull. "Na, you're stuck with us until I have me a wagon of coins and don't need ya anymore." He knew it would take the blothrud several moments to get off the ground and lunge at him, so he had plenty of time to step away if it should happen.

Leaning his body against the cool bars, he pressed his face between two of them and relaxed. "Ya got too much drive to give up. You'll fight and win against anything they throw at ya. And every time the stakes get higher, the winnings do as well."

Santorray grinned at the obese man with a cunning look that gave his captor an uneasy feeling. "I suggest you drop the keys to my cage right now and run away."

Blox smiled back. "And why would I be freeing my money maker?"

"Because it might be the only way you survive this." His grin grew even larger.

"And I suppose you're goin' ta bust me up if I don't comply."

"Nope," came Kyndra's voice from behind Blox. "We will."

JERI "RED" SHEPHERD

Veteran. #1 Bestselling Author. Game Writer.

Author | Anthology Producer Jeri "Red" Shepherd

Red, a USAF veteran living in Wisconsin, was honored to help Nerd Street's Ben Penrod build this anthology! A multi-genre author writing as Jeri Shepherd, Reji Laberje, and Maggie McMahon, she is a 15-Time #1 Bestselling, award-winning, 30-year professional creative of nearly 120 published works, focusing today on genre fiction, games, children's books, and writing resources. Alongside *Otherworldly* author TR Nickel, she co-founded Red Rose Works (RRW), which (with other authors) supports writers through masterminds, workshops, and program management at conventions nationwide. RRW also boasts the Girl Power GM duo and owns the Dungeon Race RPG game company. At the end of 2024, Red is launching the *"Yours in Writing"* podcast. She also continues in private author coaching, managing Lucy's Lantern Literature (a publishing imprint), and serving clients including *Legends of Avantris*, the *For The Love Of* brand, and content for Luke Gygax's *G20 Magazine* using her life-long writing and publishing industry experience. Connect with Red at: **linktr.ee/redwritesbooks**

CHAPTER ELEVEN

The Vampirization Of The Human Galileans – A Galilean Expedition Prequel

By: Jeri Red Shepherd

Crimson Chaos

B LOOD SPRAYED IN ERRATIC pulses, standing out starkly against the sterile white of the medical bay. Celeste's hands moved with surgical precision, her fingers weaving through the chaos, attempting to clamp down on the severed artery that threatened to end her patient's life prematurely. Around her, the crew worked frantically, their faces set in grim determination as they handed her tools and sponges.

"Pressure here!" she commanded, and a nurse pressed down where she pointed, staunching the flow momentarily.

Surgery in space was an even more fragile situation than the most grave of procedures on gravity-bound surfaces. While the medical bay was pressurized and fitted with artificial centrifugal gravity, blood flow and the human body's biological nature was never completely fooled. Open wounds wanted to stay open and each heartbeat that worked to pump blood through veins was just as likely to push it straight out of the body.

"Stay with me," Celeste murmured, not sure if the words were meant more for the patient or herself.

Her determination was a tangible force, an unyielding wall against the specter of death that loomed over the operating table. This wasn't just about saving a life; it was a fight to uphold the legacy of their mission, to prove that humanity could persevere even amidst the stars, even when facing the unknown, and even when there were so few of them left to make the journey. Every life was precious.

The monitor beeped rhythmically now. The patient's breathing steadied, and the blood flow abated, replaced by the soft hum of medical equipment and relieved sighs from the crew. Celeste's hands were steady as she sutured the wounds. But something was off. The patient's skin had turned a bluish-gray color, and blood congealed quickly on the gauze.

"Scalpel," she commanded, her voice betraying none of the curiosity that sparked within her.

She made a small incision cutting away the last suture she had just stitched. She prepared for the usual floating flow. Instead, what oozed out was sluggish and thick, pooling lethargically on the flesh. It was the exact opposite of her expectation after a lifetime of working on the human form in its space-bound existence. This was no ordinary hemorrhage. This was something else, something alien to her medical knowledge. Celeste wiped the dark substance between her gloved fingers, analyzing its consistency. She looked down at her patient and the place she had been suturing was already scabbing—the glue-like substance closing the wound off from the elements in a way that her medical mind understood would surely heal them faster. Her mind raced with hypotheses, each more bizarre than the last.

"Get me a sample container," she ordered, but her crew was preoccupied, tending to other casualties of the recent spacial turbulence that had tossed their bodies against the unforgiving metal edges of their generational ship.

Driven by a scientist's curiosity, or perhaps some unforeseen instinct, Celeste brought her finger to her lips without hesitation. The sweetness of metal flooded her senses, accompanied by a shocking realization. Iron. She could actually taste it. Anemia was often a problem amongst space-dwellers, so to find such metallically rich blood in a wounded patient was more than a little curious. Stranger still was that the taste caused her mouth to drip with insatiable yearning. She thirsted for more and the longing frightened her. Their human bodies were starving for iron out here, living off of hydroponic and imitation-UV lab-grown flora that were short of the levels of protein and minerals on which their Earth-bound ancestors once survived. Travelers grew to crave the nutrient with a carnivorous intensity that bordered on primal.

For decades, a space madness had been taking over generation ships as the travelers would turn on one another, attack, and drain the blood of their shipmates like vampires. It had prevented them from moving beyond the Galilean stop outside of Jupiter from which they would seek deeper space. In that moment, with the liquid life of Celeste's patient on her tongue, it suddenly made sense. Iron cravings explained the symptoms, the changes. The

Galilean humans, those meant to reach the first of their intergalactic travels on Jupiter's Galilean moons before venturing further into space, were adapting, transforming in response to an environment where traditional nutrients were scarce.

Just as they were to finally land on one of the minor Galilean moons, not only were they exposed to the harsh conditions of navigating the asteroids and orbiting rocks of the giant planet, but the crew's instincts had turned, threatening the vampirization to which so many before them had fallen. But what if it was never about madness? Celeste's heart hammered with the implications of her discovery. If they could harness this knowledge, understand it, they might secure their survival. They might fulfill the legacy that they had embarked upon, not just as survivors, but as pioneers of human evolution.

Evolution

Celeste's boots echoed through the hollow metal corridors, each thud a heartbeat in the silence. The sterile lights overhead flickered faintly, casting long, angular shadows that stretched like reaching fingers. There was something unnerving about the quiet, something that hummed beneath the surface like a whisper of things left unsaid. She quickened her pace, urgency driving her deeper into the labyrinth of steel and machinery, into the belly of the ship where curiosity twisted with the dark hunger she just now coming to understand.

The lab greeted her with its cold, clinical atmosphere—gleaming surfaces reflecting the harsh, artificial light. Beneath the sterility, something foul lurked, as though the very air held the weight of forgotten rituals. Celeste grabbed a sample container, its clear sides soon smeared with the thick, iron-rich substance that masqueraded as blood. It was not human . . . at least not anymore.

"Computer," she commanded, her voice sharp in the oppressive quiet. "Initiate full spectral analysis on the sample. Priority one."

"Processing," the computer responded, its calm, detached voice at odds with the storm brewing inside her.

The centrifuge clicked together with eerie precision, each component slotting into place like a puzzle she had solved too many times before. The machine whirred to life, separating the dark essence into layers, exposing truths she wasn't sure she wanted to see. Celeste's fingers danced over the microscope, adjusting the dials until the slide came into sharp focus. She leaned in, her breath shallow as she peered into the circle of light, her world narrowing to the distorted cells before her.

What she saw twisted her stomach in knots. These cells were not merely human—they were something else, something wrong. They writhed, as though alive with a will of their own, membranes stretched and distended in grotesque shapes. Iron particles clung to them, embedding themselves deep within the very core of each cell. This was no natural adaptation; it was a violent internal violation of the body's sanctity, a grotesque mockery of life as she had known it. Evolution didn't move this fast—unless something far darker had spurred it on.

Fascination warred with dread as she watched the transformation unfolding under her microscope. These cells weren't just surviving—they were thriving, becoming something more, something resilient and unbreakable. It was as if the ship itself, this cold, dead place, had birthed a new form of life, coaxed out by the void and fed by iron. The implications clawed at the edges of her mind, threatening to unravel her sanity. Who . . . *or what* were they becoming?

"Record findings," she said, her voice hard, her determination unshaken even as the chill of dread crept up her spine. "Hemoglobin synthesis appears altered, with potential for increased oxygen transportation efficiency. Hypothesis: correlation with environmental exposure to heavy iron deposits."

"Recording," the computer replied, its clinical detachment grating to Celeste who wanted another voice to reflect the concern she was experiencing.

She sent the findings to Dr. Elara, the one person who might understand, who might have already seen these dark changes unfolding. Dr. Elara had survived the vampirized ships before, though no one knew exactly how. Her escape pod had been ejected back in space toward the next generational ship and, after many months of traveling alone, she found herself on *Perdition's Promise*, the ship Celeste served. Perhaps the older scientist had seen this twisted transformation long before Celeste had. They were both tied to this now, bound by the weight of discovery, of a revelation that may not be salvation, but a descent into something far worse.

As the machine hummed, documenting what might be the first steps toward a grotesque future, Celeste felt the truth settle in her bones. This was not mere survival—they were becoming something other, something monstrous. And yet, she could not turn away from the promise of transformation. It called to her, whispered of a future where humanity was no longer bound by the frailties of flesh. They could become more—if they dared to cross the threshold.

She walked through the ship's corridors, her mind racing with the gravity of what they had discovered. The lights flickered overhead as if they, too, sensed the darkness creeping in. Finally, she reached the command deck, where Captain Anderson stood, his gaze fixed on data streams that no longer mattered.

"Captain," she said, her voice steady, though inside she quaked with anticipation. "I've discovered something . . . something that may be crucial for our survival."

Anderson turned, his face a mask of calm. He raised an eyebrow in an inviting explanation.

She handed him the data pad, her hand unwavering, though her pulse thrummed with fear. He scanned the graphs and images, his expression unreadable. The cells—twisted, aberrant—glowed on the screen, undeniable in their significance.

"Explain," he said at last, his voice low and controlled.

"The environmental conditions," Celeste began, "I don't believe they are hostile, Sir. I think they could be a catalyst for change. Our bodies are evolving, Captain. The iron-rich atmosphere is enhancing our blood's ability to carry oxygen, strengthening us. I think we could survive out here—perhaps even thrive."

"That's the hope, Doctor. We're not going to New Terra just in hopes of dying there," he said.

"No, Sir. I mean, we could survive out here . . . in space. Maybe even on the Galilean Moon when we land there. I think we're evolving," she responded.

Beside the captain, Lieutenant Alexei frowned, his dark eyes narrowing in suspicion. "Evolution doesn't happen overnight," he said, his voice cutting into their conversation. Celeste hadn't known he'd heard them. "How can you be sure?" he asked.

She met his gaze without flinching. "The samples show accelerated adaptation. My patient was healing within minutes of my having treated his wound. If we don't explore this, we risk extinction."

"Or worse," Anderson said, his tone edged with unease. "Uncontrolled mutation. Disease. Are you ready to gamble with the lives of this crew, Dr. Celeste?"

"It's not a gamble," she replied, her resolve like the iron about which she spoke. "It's a calculated risk. Without this change, we'll die out here."

"You don't know that!" Alexei said defensively.

"Every other ship has!" she shot back.

"And how do we know your experiments won't be the death sentence?" Alexei pressed, his voice taut with tension. "What if that's what happened to the other ships that made it this far?"

"Failsafes," she promised. "I'll put them in place. I'll protect us."

The silence on the command deck deepened, the hum of the ship growing louder, as if the walls themselves were holding their breath. Finally, Anderson nodded, though his reluctance was palpable.

"You're asking us to change our very biology," he said, his voice heavy with the weight of the unknown.

"It's the only way," Celeste replied, her conviction unshaken. "We must become the architects of our own evolution."

"You mean play God . . . literally!" said the lieutenant.

"In a place that treats our bodies godlessly, shouldn't somebody?" she asked.

The captain's eyes narrowed as he stared into the void beyond the ship's hull, where the unknown awaited. After a long pause, he spoke, his voice a whisper in the dark. "Alright, Dr. Celeste. I'll give you the resources. But I want protocols. If anything goes wrong—"

"Nothing will go wrong," Celeste interrupted, her voice firm. "I have someone who can guide us through this."

"Who?" Anderson asked, a flicker of curiosity breaking through his stoicism.

"Dr. Elara," Celeste said, her pulse quickening. "She's seen this before."

And with that, the shadows of their future loomed even darker.

Survival

Celeste returned to the patient she had saved, the breathing was steady but alien. The bluish-gray skin now seemed like a signpost towards humanity's ability to endure any environment in the universe. With Dr. Elara's guidance, Celeste knew they would delve into uncharted scientific territories. The risks were great, but so were the possibilities. If they could harness this transformation, they could might the possibility of adaptation and survival for generations to come.

"Humanity's evolution will not be stopped by space," Celeste mused, echoing Dr. Elara's teachings.

The med bay's doors slid open with a hiss as Celeste stepped out, ready to begin work with the enigmatic Dr. Elara in their lab. Elara stood in the doorway like a relic from another world—her figure gaunt, skin drawn tight over sharp bones, and eyes that seemed to absorb the very light around her.

The rumors whispered through the ship about her time aboard *The Orpheus*, a ship whose crew had turned on one another, consuming flesh in a madness born of starvation and isolation. Elara alone had emerged from that nightmare, untouched by death's hand but marked by something deeper. Her gaze carried a hollowness, as if the void had seeped into her soul, a cold, endless hunger lingering behind her measured movements. Her presence was unnerving—a constant reminder of the fine line between survival and the abyss. Most let her to her own isolation, alive but not really living aboard Perdition's Promise. Celeste knew that engaging the woman's knowledge was the only way forward.

Dr. Elara peered through the microscope, anticipation making her breath shallow. The magnified blood cells were misshapen yet full of potential.

"Look at this," Dr. Elara said in awe. "The iron compound—it's not just sustaining them; it's changing them."

Celeste nodded, "It's as if we're witnessing a rapid evolution. These cells are adapting at an alarming rate."

They documented each observation, their hands steady despite the gravity of their findings. Data spilled across screens and printouts, revealing a future where human limitations could be surpassed. But with revelation came dilemma. Celeste and Dr. Elara faced ethical quandaries in their quest to replace life's essence with liquid iron. The choices made within these walls would determine humanity's legacy.

"Are we ready for this?" Celeste asked, breaking the silence . . . her gaze met Dr. Elara's, searching for certainty in the scientist's weathered face.

"Readiness is a luxury," Dr. Elara replied, her tone measured. "Survival is the necessity. But we must consider the consequences. We are altering the core of our being."

"Yet, isn't adaptation our greatest strength?" Celeste countered. "To endure, to overcome—that's the mark we leave behind."

"At what cost?" Dr. Elara pressed her lips together, contemplating the moral weight of their endeavor. "We risk losing what makes us human."

"Or we gain the means to thrive where no human has before," Celeste insisted. "This is our chance to carve a path through the stars, to ensure our species endures beyond the cradle of Earth."

Dr. Elara sighed, the burden of decision etching lines deeper into her face. "Then proceed, but with caution. Our actions now will echo through generations. We have to tread carefully, lest we lose ourselves in the process."

"Agreed," Celeste said. She turned back to the samples, her resolve hardened by the promise of discovery. Then, cautiously, "Did you disocver this on *The Orpheus?*"

After a pause, "I wish I had," Dr. Elara said.

And so, they worked through the cycle of hours, compiling evidence, challenging hypotheses, and inching closer to a truth that would redefine what it meant to be human. Routine reports to Captain Anderson were part of the path to discover the transformation at least as quickly as it beckoned.

"Captain," Celeste began, "We need to discuss the implications of the transformation."

Anderson turned from the stars, his face a mask of command worn by years of navigating the unknown. "I've read Dr. Elara's report. You're requesting to alter the very biology of our crew."

"Correct," Celeste affirmed. "The liquid iron compound could be the key to surviving environments we can't even imagine."

Risks and benefits hung between them like a scale awaiting judgment. The captain considered the weight of each decision as if the lives of his crew dangled on either side.

"The risks?" Alexei prompted tersely.

"Unknown psychological effects, potential dependency on the compound, rejection by some of the crew's bodies," she listed without flinching.

"And the benefits?" asked the Captain.

"Enhanced oxygen transport, resistance to radiation, resistance to Kelvin extremes, possibly extending life spans under duress," Celeste replied. "Put more simply, oxygen becomes far less necessary. Body temperatures can drop to levels never before imagined. Even gravitational changes would have less effect on our ability to survive."

"And how do you imagine proceeding," asked the captain.

"My patient," she said. "I would like to create more of the compound and inject him with it. He's already got some circulating in his body, so it's not foreign to his system. This would be an extension of what he's already been experiencing."

"Proceed with caution. And with his permission," Anderson decided after a heavy silence. "I don't want this forced on anybody for any reason. And I want continuous monitoring. Any sign of adverse reactions, and we halt the experiment."

"Understood." Celeste nodded, acknowledging the dangers.

Lab Rats

Celeste and Dr. Elara were once more in the lab, surrounded by the hum of machines and sterile scents. Their eyes flicked toward the volunteer strapped into the medical chair behind them, pale skin reflecting the cold glow of the overhead lights. The subject's veins had been prepared for the injection—a series of tubes running from an intravenous drip, feeding into a clear vial that housed the iron compound. The liquid within shimmered faintly, almost unnaturally dense, with a metallic sheen that caught the light in an unsettling way. It was no ordinary iron; it had been specially synthesized to bond directly with the hemoglobin, promising transformation at a cellular level.

With careful precision, Celeste guided a mechanical injector toward her patient's arm. The sterile needle, long and narrow, gleamed as it hovered above the skin. The faint hiss of machinery was the only sound as it pierced the surface, slipping into the vein like a blade sliding through silk. For a brief moment, the volunteer's breath hitched, the body instinctively recoiling from the foreign intrusion.

"Beginning transfusion," Celeste announced, her voice steady despite the tension thickening in the room.

The iron compound began to flow, dark and viscous, snaking through the clear tubing toward the subject's bloodstream. As it entered, the volunteer's veins darkened, the iron spread rapidly beneath the pale skin like ink spilling across a page. The change was immediate—subtle at first, but soon the volunteer's breathing quickened, and his heart rate spiked on the monitors as the compound took hold.

The liquid coursed through the body, binding with the red blood cells, altering them at their core. As it integrated, the skin around the injection site began to cool, a bluish tint creeping outward like a spider's web, signaling the transformation already underway. The volunteer's eyelids fluttered, muscles twitching involuntarily as the compound spread through the circulatory system.

Celeste and Elara watched with silent intensity. The blood cells on the screen warped and shifted as the iron bonded to them, reshaping their structure with alarming efficiency. The volunteer groaned softly, caught in the throes of transformation.

"The body's rejecting it," Celeste muttered, her hand hovering over the console to halt the process.

"Wait," Dr. Elara commanded, her voice sharp. "It's adapting."

Moments later, the violent reaction began to subside, and the volunteer's vitals evened out. The skin, once blue-tinged, began to settle into an ashen pallor as the compound fully integrated into their system. A new kind of calm fell over the room—a silence laden with dark anticipation.

The first phase of the transformation was complete.

Together, they examined altered blood cells under the microscope. Their eyes had grown tired with the repeated effort, but it was the only way to move forward.

"Look at the cellular integrity," Dr. Elara pointed out, a restrained excitement in her tone. "It's unprecedented."

"Imagine the applications," Celeste mused, her mind ablaze with the ramifications. Each discovery brought them closer to a legacy defined not by the frailties of flesh and bone but by the indomitable will to evolve.

They worked tirelessly, recording every change and reaction. Their pursuit was driven by the belief that each finding would lead to something bigger. As time passed, Celeste's focus shifted to the transformation. It was no longer just about survival - it was about leaving a lasting legacy in their very cells.

In one of her routine check-ins, Celeste prepared to share the findings of her experiments. The metal door slid open with a hiss, and the doctor strode into Captain Anderson's quarters without the customary hesitation.

"Captain," she began, her voice laced with an urgency that bordered on desperation, "It's not just an experiment anymore. This is a liquid iron that can mimic our very blood."

"Explain," he commanded, his eyes locked onto hers. His voice was a calm contrast to the storm of thoughts surely raging in his mind.

"Under extreme conditions, it sustains cellular function, carries oxygen that stays in the body. It's stable." Celeste's hands moved animatedly as she spoke, outlining the potential of her discovery in the dim light of the cabin. "If we can adapt this to our physiology, we might survive out here, beyond the reach of our solar system."

"Survive." Captain Anderson repeated the word like a mantra. He let it hang in the air between them, a life raft in a sea of uncertainty. To leave a part of humanity etched into the fabric of the cosmos—they could become undying pioneers in the starry ocean.

They were on the cusp of redefining existence itself, reshaping their destiny on the anvil of necessity. Celeste knew the risks, but the allure of forging a new path for humanity was irresistible.

"It's time to tell the crew," he said.

"Thank you, Captain."

Vampirization

The sterile light of the conference room bathed the faces of those assembled. Captain Anderson stood at the head of the table, his posture rigid under the weight of their future. Beside him, Celeste scanned the gathered crew with a critical eye. They were chosen for their expertise and willingness to embrace the unknown.

Dr. Elara, her mentor, entered last. The air seemed to shift, anticipation crackling like static as she took her place. She was a figure carved from the cold void of space itself; her reputation as an exobiology expert was as much a part of her as her own DNA.

"Thank you all for coming," Celeste began, her voice cutting cleanly through the quiet. "This is Dr. Elara for those who have not had the honor of meeting her. She has guided my understanding of transformative biology."

Dr. Elara nodded, her gaze sweeping across the tentative faces. "Our goal," she stated, "is survival. But not just clinging to life—rather, we want to evolve to conquer it."

Her plan was laid bare with clinical precision. A wider group of volunteers would submit to the integration of the liquid iron compound into their systems. It was uncharted territory, a frontier lined with shadows and fraught with peril.

Celeste helped with the setup, displaying human anatomy and simulations of the compound. The volunteers sat in their chairs, determined to fulfill their mission. They were the first pieces of Dr. Elara's vision - a new lineage born from determination and necessity. Each volunteer underwent a similar experience to the first patient: jarring, frightening, but ultimately not life-ending.

Dr. Elara and Celeste worked together, eyes glued to the monitors displaying live data while each took shifts. The cold screen light cast shadows on their faces, revealing every subtle reaction as they watched the transformations taking place inside the subjects' bodies. Heart rates increased, blood pressure rose, and body temperatures spiked in testament to the profound changes happening within them before plunging back down to hypothermic levels.

"Document everything," Dr. Elara commanded in one of their shared shifts, her voice betraying no emotion. Celeste complied, her hands steady despite the maelstrom of anxiety within her. She recorded each tremor, each bead of sweat that formed on the volunteers' brows, adding grim annotations to the clinical data.

As hours turned into days, the crew's transformation became evident. Skin paled to an alabaster sheen; eyes darkened, mirroring the void outside the ship's hull. They spoke of a thirst that water could not quench—a gnawing emptiness that begged for iron, for the lifeblood that the compound mimicked.

"Find a solution," Dr. Elara instructed, her gaze never wavering from her charges. "We cannot afford chaos."

Celeste nodded. They searched the ship's inventory for any source of the precious element. They created supplements from spare parts, rationing doses of liquid iron for survival. The volunteer crewmembers lined up to receive their allotment with a mix of gratitude and dread.

"Remember why we're doing this," Dr. Elara said, her voice cutting through Celeste's reverie. "We adapt, or we perish."

Their next experiment was to mimic the very Galilean minor moon on which they were to set down before going forth into even deeper space. The volunteers by this point were more human-like than human. Their skin was grayish blue and hardened. Their eyes were dark and empty. They still spoke and moved like themselves, though their strength seemed fortified by the metal within. The group entered a sealed bay nervously without the usual exterior protection of suits and dome helmets worn when on hull duties.

"Initiating Galilean atmospheric conditions," Celeste announced from a control room.

The chamber hissed, sucking out all of the oxygen little by little. The volunteers seemed to not notice. Then, the room rumbled, simulating the violent storms and crushing pressures of the gas giant. Inside, the volunteers braced themselves, but stayed erect. Against all biological understanding, they were doing well.

Celeste and Dr. Elara watched the readouts, minutes felt like hours. Body temperatures were Kelvinic, but stable, heart rates were elevated but steady. The liquid iron coursing through their veins had transformed them, making them able to survive in lethal environments.

Survival on the minor moon, a barren rock orbiting Jupiter, became a tangible possibility. It was no longer just a waypoint; it could be home.

Old Blood

Gathered around the conference table were the volunteers who had allowed the compound into their bodies, Dr. Elara, and Captain Anderson as Celeste laid out the discoveries.

"Our original destination offers a gentler environment, yes," she said. "But our people are weary of travel. We believe that, on our moon base, we can survive—not just survive. We can live here. Make it a home."

Dr. Elara added. "It's not about what's easy. It's about what makes us evolve, what pushes us beyond our limits."

"We could stop traveling. We don't even know what lies beyond this refurbishing point in space," Celeste added.

Arguments broke out, voices raised in concern and excitement. Some feared the unknowns of a permanent settlement on such a hostile world. Others argued for the potential of what they could become, the allure of becoming a species that could claim even the harshest corners of space.

"Remember why we embarked on this journey," Celeste reminded them, her voice a beacon amidst the storm of debate. "To forge a path for humanity, wherever it may lead."

The volunteers, prior to the experiments, had been fitted with physiological monitors that fed to readouts on wrist-mounted devices that Celeste watched. In the midst of the conversations in the conference room, alarms started beeping. First one, then another, and another. Each of the volunteers began to fade in energy, before becoming enraged, mad, ravenous. Celeste ran to a monitor on one of the walls and keyed in a few strokes. The numbers were dropping faster than expected, causing alarm as she cross-referenced data streams.

"Dr. Elara," Celeste called out, voice crisp in the sterile air of the lab. "The iron levels—they're dropping."

The older scientist joined Celeste at the console, seeking confirmation of the bad news.

"Impossible," Dr. Elara murmured, though the evidence was stark against the glow of the screen. "Unless . . . "

"Unless someone has interfered," Celeste finished, dread pooling in her stomach.

As one of the volunteers leapt across the conference room table, Celeste managed to push a few buttons on her wrist and all of the volunteers went unconscious just as the Captain found himself in the hungry grasp of one of his own crew. Captain Anderson watched as the vampirized volunteer clumped down in sleep upon the table before having gained access to his blood.

"My failsafe, Sir," Celeste breathed. "They're okay. Just sleeping. I wanted to ensure our safety as we experimented."

"We should end this," he said.

"No, Captain," Dr. Elara jumped in. "This madness, it's their old human form. Their old blood. That's what it's always been. They need the iron in the compound. If we have that in our bodies, the madness won't come. We need to find out why the levels have dropped. We affixed timed injections to them and it looks like their devices have not given them the last two doses. If we fix that issue, Sir , we fix them. And, moreover, we prevent ourselves from becoming just like them."

The captain and scientists split up, moving with purpose through the ship's corridors. They navigated the maze of technology and shadows. Celeste found Alexei in the lab, his hands moving with deft grace as he bypassed safety protocols. Adrenaline sharpened her senses as she stepped into the room.

"Alexei!" The name burst from her lips, carrying the weight of accusation.

He spun around, his expression a mix of guilt and defiance. "You don't under-stand," he said, a tremble in his voice. "We can't stay here—it's a death sentence. You are all dead. You're turning us into the dead. The undead! Vampires!"

"You're sentencing us all if you stop these experiments, Alexei. We must adapt or we will die. Space has decided to change us. But if we don't help it along, we may very well perish."

"This blood. It's not human. It's not who we are," he said.

"It's who we are becoming, Alexei!" Celeste shouted.

Dr. Elara arrived, breathless, just in time to hear the exchange. Her disap-pointment was a palpable thing, filling the space between them.

"Alexei," she said quietly, "your fears are clouding your judgment."

"Think of what we will become if we let fear dictate our actions!" Celeste shouted.

The standoff lasted only moments more before the captain appeared in the lab. His expression hardened and Alexei's shoulders slumped, his resolve crumbling. He relinquished control of the system, stepping back into the grasp of Dr. Elara, who held him with a firm but gentle grip. But something in his expression told Celeste he may yet try to stand in the way of progress.

"Let's fix this," Celeste said, her voice steady despite the chaos that threatened to unravel within her. Together, they worked to reverse the sabotage, restoring the flows and checks that kept the lifeblood of the volunteers, the liquid iron, circulating through their veins.

Descent

Two weeks of navigating the orbiting asteroids and minor moons of Jupiter finally led Captain Anderson to a surface he felt was worthy of landing their ship full of travelers. They weren't the same humans who had been born in space, children of the Earth-bound visionaries who had set out in search of a new deep-space colony. The blood of their ancestors had been drained, replaced with the iron compound that made them a new species. Resilient. Powerful. And yet unknown even to themselves.

As they landed on the minor Galilean moon, they set to work, their vampire-like speed and iron-forged strength making quick progress. Structures slowly rose from the cargo areas that held the terraforming necessities originally meant for a much different environment. Each beam and panel was placed with a determination that spoke of more than mere survival. Their legacy would not be written in the annals of a distant Earth, but in the life they carved out here, on this minor moon, where humanity's tenacity and their newfound nature converged.

Celeste descended the ramp from the ship. The silence of the Galilean atmosphere surrounded her. The weight of her exogeological equipment was a comforting presence as she took her first step onto the lunar dust, marking the start of a new chapter. The air was thin and bit into her lungs, a reminder of the moon's unforgiving nature. She drew the frigid breath deep into her chest, feeling it cut through her with a precision that matched the clarity of her purpose, awed at her physiology's very workings. She scanned the barren, desolate landscape. This would be their legacy - etched into the very fabric of the universe.

As her gaze lingered on the rough terrain, Celeste felt a surge of iron-hardened exhilaration pulse through her veins. There was work to be done, knowledge to be uncovered. She stood ready to carve understanding from the cold stone of this alien world. Her duty beckoned, a siren call to the scientist within, urging her to contribute to the collective memory of her vampiric kin.

They would thrive here, in this stark landscape, and forge a new life—not in spite of their vampiric nature, but because of it. Humanity's legacy would persist, not through flesh and bone, but through spirit and will, metal-blooded humans in this alien world.

The human colony wasn't going anywhere. The minor Galilean moon was home.

Watch for *Galilean Origins* coming soon. The eye of Jupiter is failing. Stakes are high: moon collisions, altered rotations, magnetic disturbances and sickness threaten Galilean life. Seven Galileans from as many moons and Galilean races—a commander, pilot, engineer, meteorologist, strategist, geologist, and doctor—embark on a mission to stabilize Jupiter. The first book of the *Galilean Expedition* duology introduces this diverse crew as they prepare for the perilous journey ahead while the second, *Galilean Mission*, sees the team face trials and tribulations as they seek to calm the storm. Watch also for TTRPGs set in the world.

NERD STREET

BEN PENROD

All of the authors in this collection attend one or many of the *Nerd Street* events around the United States. *Nerd Street* is an event production company started and operated by Ben Penrod. Ben is the founder of Awesome Con, Twin Cities Con, Des Moines Con, Madison Comic & Pop Culture Expo, Central Florida Comic Con, Annapolis Comic-Con, Southern Maryland Comic-Con, Sugoi Expo, and co-founder of Alaska ComicCon.

Ben was obsessed with comics and cartoons from a young age and—in the late '90s—began selling parts of his collection on eBay . . . and used the money to buy even more comics on eBay. His hobby turned into a full-time job in 2008 when Ben started an online comic book store and traveled the country selling comics at conventions. Ben joined Steve Anderson from *Third Eye Comics* to create the Annapolis Comic-Con in 2011, soon followed by the Southern Maryland Comic-Con, and both are still thriving local shows that cater to comic book lovers like themselves. In 2013, Ben launched Awesome Con in Washington, DC. It was an immediate success and quickly grew into one of the largest fan conventions in the United States.

Ben stepped back from actively managing Awesome Con in 2018, and--in 2019--started Central Florida Comic Con in Lakeland, Florida. In 2020, with longtime friend Brett Carreras (from Virginia ComiCon), Ben started Alaska ComiCon in Fairbanks, Alaska. Twin Cities Con was added to the list of Nerd Street events in 2021, and 2022 saw the debuts of Des Moines Con and Sugoi Expo in Orlando. In 2024, Madison Comic & Pop Culture Expo also joined the list of events produced by Nerd Street. Learn more at:

www.nerdstreetusa.com/

Made in the USA
Middletown, DE
21 May 2025